Jill has two ponies

This is the third 'Jill' book. In *Jill's gymkhana*
she learned to ride her first pony, and in
A stable for Jill she set up a hacking stable.
Now Jill buys a second pony, Rapide, a bay,
but she very much regrets her rash decision,
because she thinks that Rapide has taken an
instant dislike to her. But she perseveres
with him and together they learn new riding
skills, including helping to run a riding
school, until in the end Rapide is as much a
part of the family as Black Boy,
Jill's first pony.

Ask your local bookseller, or at your public
library, for details of other Knight Books, or
write to the Editor-in-Chief, Knight
Books, Arlen House, Salisbury Road,
Leicester LE1 7QS

Ruby Ferguson

Jill has two ponies

Illustrated by Bonar Dunlop

KNIGHT BOOKS

the paperback division of Brockhampton Press

FOR PRISCILLA

SBN 340 04142 0

This edition first published 1968 by Knight Books,
the paperback division of Brockhampton Press Ltd,
Leicester
Second impression 1970

Printed and bound in Great Britain by
Cox & Wyman Ltd, London, Reading and Fakenham

First published by Hodder and Stoughton Ltd 1952
Fifth impression 1962
Illustrations copyright © 1968 Brockhampton Press
Ltd

Contents

1 - I meet Rapide

'HERE is Rapide,' said Mrs. Penberthy, briskly leading out a bay pony. 'Look, he has taken to your little girl at once!'

From my point of view there were several things wrong with these remarks. In the first place, Rapide is a silly name for a pony unless it is going to be in a circus; in the second place, I think it is insulting to refer to a person of fourteen as though she were six; and in the third place, Rapide far from taking to me at once had given me a very dirty look out of his rather disagreeable eyes. The fact was, I didn't like Mrs. Penberthy, I didn't like Rapide, and I didn't know what I was going to do about it. I was worried, because Mummy would be so upset if she knew, after going to all that trouble to get me a show jumper.

Those of you who have read my previous book, *A stable for Jill*, will remember that by devious ways I had amassed the sum of sixty pounds to buy myself a second pony, and that Mummy had met some people on the boat coming from America who had just the very pony for me that they wanted to sell because their daughter had grown out of him. I was naturally excited about this pony because he was said to have

7

done awfully well for the Penberthy girl, and for nights before we went to Little Grazings, which was the peculiar name of the Penberthys' house, I dreamed about a pony beautiful to look at and wonderful in action.

So in the end Mummy fixed a Saturday with Mrs. Penberthy and we went down by train, which took about an hour and a half. Mummy read a book in the train as calmly as if we were going to do some mere shopping – I don't know how grown-ups can *be* like that – and I fidgeted about and pulled at my gloves and felt like rushing madly up and down the corridor to work off some of my pent-up emotion, and Mummy kept giving me a look which said as plainly as anything, need you let everybody in the carriage think you are completely bats?

I then began to feel sorry for the rest of the people in our carriage because they were obviously not on their way to buy show jumpers but were just having to make this journey for some horribly mere purposes. I hope you will not mind me using the word 'mere' again so soon, but it is such a grey sort of word that I think it expresses all the dreary things that grown-up people do all the time, like seeing lawyers and having treatments and meeting people for lunch that they used to know about forty years ago.

There was a woman opposite me who was probably going to meet somebody for lunch, and the man next to me looked as if he was to have a treatment, and the younger man next to Mummy was obviously going to see a lawyer because he kept turning over a lot of typewritten papers and gnawing his thumb nail. I thought I was getting quite detective-ish, and then just for fun I started picturing those people mounted on ponies and it was so funny I gave a snort – like you do when you try not to giggle – and Mummy gave me more of a look than ever, so I went very quiet and stared out of the window giving myself marks for fields that had horses in them and taking off marks for empty fields or just cows.

So from this you will have an idea what I felt like all the way to the Penberthys', and how worked up I was when we got there and Mrs. Penberthy opened the loose box and the pony was actually before my eyes.

Now you had better go back to the beginning of this book and read the first bit again. I looked at Rapide and Rapide looked at me, and we just didn't register at all. I felt like you do when you miss the vaulting horse at gym and land on the mat sitting down and the form giggles and you have got a crush on the gym mistress and want her to think you are marvellous.

I couldn't say a word, of course, because it seemed so rude and ungrateful, and Mrs. Penberthy had been so nice – until she made the silly remark I have recorded – and had given us coffee.

So I thought I would put it all into my face like they do on the films. I put it all into my face and looked at Mummy hard, hoping she would understand, but I can't be very good at expressions, as she told me afterwards that how I looked was as if I had been struck dumb with joy.

When she had looked at me she looked at Mrs. Penberthy who was hanging on to Rapide's halter as if she thought he would go up in the air, and said, 'I can see that Jill is quite overcome with excitement, Mrs. Penberthy. He does look an awfully nice pony and so well groomed. But what we are interested in is his jumping. Do you think we could see him in action?'

'Oh, of course,' said Mrs. Penberthy. 'I'm sure you'll be delighted with him. Joan has been riding him in the under-sixteens for two seasons and has taken so many prizes and cups we hardly know where to put them. She wouldn't think of parting with Rapide except that now she is seventeen she's out of the pony classes. We are going to get her a hunter for Christmas. But she adores Rapide and I'm sure she'll be heart-broken when he goes.'

I felt like saying, far be it from me to break the heart of even Joan Penberthy, but Mrs. Penberthy went on, 'How old are you, Jill?'

'Fourteen,' I said.

'Ah, a lovely age for riding,' she went on. 'You still have two years in the children's classes. I'm sure Joan wishes she was fourteen again.'

I thought Joan must be a very funny person if she did, as it was the dream of my life to be seventeen and have a hunter, but I didn't say anything because as you go through life you find some people have the weirdest ideas and think them quite right and Joan might be one of those.

All this time Rapide was looking at me with the

greatest disdain as if I wasn't a bit what he had
expected, and I was trying not to look at him at all
only I was sort of fascinated like they say rabbits are
by snakes. I wish I knew if this is true.

'We'll have to wait till Joan comes in,' said Mrs.
Penberthy. 'She's gone down to the post office on
her bike.'

She pushed Rapide back into the loose box as if she
was putting a lawn-mower away, and Mummy stood
smiling as much as to say, 'How marvellous everything is', and I just stood. I think Mrs. Penberthy
thought I was a bit dim, and I was surprised that
Mummy didn't notice I hadn't much to say because
I usually talk like mad all the time, only of course she
had got the impression I was dumb with bliss.

I noticed that the Penberthys had a lovely big yard
and four loose boxes. It was just the sort of place I
should have liked for myself.

'Oh, here she is at last!' cried Mrs. Penberthy and
Joan came round the corner of the house pushing her
bike. She was a very large, meek-looking girl with
spots and sticking-out teeth – I have noticed that
people with sticking-out teeth are often good at
jumping – and she was dressed in breeches and stock-
ings with turnover tops and a fawn pullover and a
shirt with rolled up sleeves and a green tie, and she
had very short straight hair fastened out of her eyes
with a grip. I took a dislike to her.

'Come and speak to Mrs. Crewe and Jill, dear,'
said her mother. 'They've come about Rapide.'

Joan came and shook hands and said, 'Hullo' and

then pulled a khaki handkerchief out of her breeches'
pocket and started twiddling it about as if she didn't
know what to do next. I knew just how she felt, as I
would have felt the same.

'Don't stand there, dear,' said Mrs. Penberthy.
'Get Rapide saddled and show Jill what he can do.'

I must say Joan was very good with Rapide, and
when he was saddled he looked very nice, only I
couldn't make myself take to him however hard I
tried, and he just glanced at me in the most contemp-
tuous way as much as to say, 'Who on earth do you
think you are?'

'I'm miles too big for him,' said Joan, and when
she was mounted her feet could have practically met
round his girths, if you know what I mean, but she
had a nice seat in spite of being so large and bulgy,
and we went into a paddock next to the yard and Joan
walked, trotted, cantered, and finally galloped Rapide
for us to see.

Rapide was obviously a very efficient pony with no
nonsense about him. In the paddock were six pro-
fessional-looking jumps and I was very envious and
wished I had them at home.

'Could we see him jump,' I managed to say huskily,
and Mrs. Penberthy nearly leapt out of her skin at
hearing me come out of my trance, so to speak.

'Of course, dear,' she said delightedly. 'Joan, put
him round the jumps. Now you're going to see
something,' she added, only I wasn't listening because
I think people who call you dear the first time they
meet you are the very depths.

So Joan on Rapide went round the jumps, a clear round. The jumps were three foot, three foot six, and four foot six.

Mrs. Penberthy beamed and said, 'There!' Mummy didn't say anything but she looked very impressed, and I just thought that Rapide had the weirdest action I ever saw in a pony.

He got over the jumps all right, but he did it in such a funny way. First he dashed at the jump, then checked completely for all the world as though he was going to refuse, then he made his mind up, popped up his forelegs, bucked up his middle, popped up his hind-legs, and he was over. He looked exactly like a rocking-horse, and quite frankly I thought he looked awful and like a very cheap, ungraceful rocking-horse. At the very idea of myself popping over the jumps at Chatton Show on Rapide I went cold in my middle. But of course I was bound to admit that he did it. He got over, and to people like Mrs. Penberthy and Mummy who didn't really know anything about equitation, and to Joan who seemed to be a person who didn't care what she looked like anyway, he was probably marvellous. And as Mrs. Penberthy said, he had won cartloads of prizes and cups, though I hope I will never have such a mere mind as to make that my main object in riding.

'He does look good,' said Mummy. 'Now do you think Jill might try him?'

Here was the moment I dreaded. Of course I had come in my jodhpurs all ready for the fray, so Joan got down and I got up, conscious that Rapide was tightening every muscle with loathing at contact with my hated form. (I expect this was all imagination, but anyway I did imagine it and it didn't make me very happy.)

I rode him round the paddock and at least he responded to my aids. He had been well schooled.

'Now try the jumps, Jill,' cried Mummy, and I went cold all over as I could tell from her voice that she meant, 'Just show these people how good you are.' I have found from talking to my friends that I am not alone in having a mother who does this sort of thing to one. If you are a person whose mother thinks you are the world's wonder because you have got a first in the Musical Chairs for under-fourteens, and gives you a sort of boiled look of pride from the rails that makes your blood run cold, then you will know what I mean. Because the great thing about riding is that you must never, never think you're marvellous, because there is always much more for you to learn, and anyway your riding is only a little bit of all the good horsemanship throughout the world, which should make you humble.

If you have read my previous books you will have heard about a girl called Susan Pyke who thought she was terrific on a pony, and of some of the things that happened to her, and you will doubtless be hearing of her again before I have finished writing this book because she is always cropping up in my life.

However, I couldn't say anything but okay to Mummy, and shutting my eyes and setting my teeth I gathered up the reins, gripped Rapide with my heels

to show him that I knew what I was doing, and set him at the first of Joan Penberthy's jumps. He refused it. Three times.

He must have done that round of jumps dozens of times. He could have done it blindfolded. But to make a long story short, with me up, the jumps he didn't refuse he walked right through. It was too awful for words. I sat there thinking of all the terrible fates that I could bring myself to wish for Rapide, like pulling a miserable old rag-and-bones man's cart, or being sold to Susan Pyke who had been ordered out of the ring several times for using the whip too much.

I couldn't sit there for ever, so I rode slowly up to where Mummy and the two Penberthys were waiting and for a minute there was a deathly hush. Mummy was obviously mortified – for which I felt sorry but I couldn't help it – and Mrs. Penberthy and Joan just as obviously thought I had never tried to jump before.

'You'll soon get into it,' said Joan kindly. 'I expect you'll be having some lessons soon.'

Mummy looked at me in reproachful silence beyond words, and Mrs. Penberthy said briskly, 'Well, Jill has seen what the pony *can* do and I wouldn't be surprised if she's as good as Joan by the time the Pony Shows come round.'

She said it as if she would be very surprised indeed, and at that moment I made up my mind that I was going to buy Rapide if only to let him see that he couldn't beat me. I suppose it was silly, but if you have read my previous books you will know that most of the things I do are silly but often turn out all right.

Mummy suddenly gulped and found her tongue, and said, 'Well – wh – wh – what about it, Jill?'

'I'm going to have him,' I said.

Mummy went red with relief and Mrs. Penberthy and Joan started beaming and telling me that Rapide would never let me down and I'd make a rider yet, and they could have got far more than sixty pounds for him if they'd sent him to Tattersalls but all they cared about was knowing the home he was going to, and far from looking broken-hearted Joan began to whistle 'Thank U Very Much' and we all went in the house and Mummy wrote out the cheque.

Mrs. Penberthy said, 'Won't you stay and have lunch?' but you can always tell by the way people say this whether they really want you to or not, and Mrs. Penberthy obviously didn't want us to but was only being polite. So Mummy said, 'Oh no, but it is very kind of you to ask us,' and after we had made arrangements for Rapide to be sent in a horse-box to Chatton station we all shook hands, and the Penberthys went out of my life for ever.

2 - Oh, why did I buy him?

When Mummy and I got to the station we found we had twenty minutes to wait for our train, and as we were both practically starving we went into the refreshment room and had some pink imitation meat sandwiches and very chipped cups of tea. Mummy said to the girl at the counter, 'Have you any cigarettes, please?' but she just said coldly, 'No cigarettes,' though about five minutes later a young man came in and I saw her give him a packet of Player's from under the counter.

'What on earth was the matter with you, Jill?' Mummy asked.

'Nothing,' I mumbled.

'I suppose you were just trying to be different from Joan. It was very silly of you. I don't understand you at all.'

'How true!' I thought concerning the last remark.

'But I could see you were thrilled with the pony,' went on Mummy. 'He's a very good pony, isn't he?'

'Oh yes,' I said. 'I'm not very taken with the name.'

'You could change that.'

'Ponies don't like having their names changed,' I said, being awkward. 'He can be Rapide if he wants. I don't really care.'

'You're making yourself over-excited,' said Mummy.

'You always get irritable when you're over-excited.'

We got into the train and opposite me was a man reading a new copy of *Horse and Hound* which is a paper you have to order, and I simply can't afford it.

I tried to read the back part which was all I could see, but Mummy nudged me and gave me a look.

Just then another man came into our carriage from the corridor and said, 'What on earth are you reading, old chap?'

'Oh, just something I picked up off the seat. It's not my line at all,' said the depraved and unappreciating man who was holding that marvellous paper.

'Well, we're nearly at our station,' said the first man, and soon the train stopped and they started collecting their things.

But my man still hung on to the paper for which I yearned and which was not his line at all. I gripped my thumbs till it hurt and simply willed him to put it down and leave it, but he didn't.

'Have you got everything, old man?' said the other man.

'Oh yes, I think so. There seems to be an awful lot.'

Oh please, please put it down! I thought.

Besides *Horse and Hound* he had the handles of two cases in the same hand. He began to get out of the carriage. He got right out and turned round to shut the door but he couldn't because he was carrying so much.

Put it down! I prayed. Oh please, please, put it down!

At the very last minute he suddenly looked at *Horse*

and Hound as if he didn't know it was there, and contemptuously flung it back on the carriage seat. In about one second I grabbed it and clutched it to my heart.

'Really, Jill!' said Mummy.

But I didn't care. I buried myself in *Horse and Hound* till we got to Chatton and then folded it up and took it home to read again in bed.

When we got home we found a lovely fire and our tea laid and the kettle simmering on the hob, which had been done for us before she left by our daily help, Mrs. Crosby, or N.R.T.B. as I call her meaning No Relation To Bing which is what she says directly she meets anybody new.

'I'll make some toast,' said Mummy. 'Meanwhile you'd better go and tell Black Boy he's going to have a brother.'

I rushed out to my little paddock, half of which is an orchard. The minute my pony saw me he came cantering to me, his beautiful eyes alight with joy, and I hurled my arms around his neck and hugged him. I loved him so much, and after all that had happened that day I felt as if I wanted to howl one terrific great howl, but I choked it down. I even felt a bit annoyed with Mummy for not understanding what I meant when I made faces at Rapide, so at the moment I decided that I cared more for Black Boy than for anybody in the world, and I wished I had a colossal amount of money – about a hundred pounds – so that he and I could ride away all by ourselves and live on an island and do exactly what we liked for ever.

I then came all over practical again, and forgetting my own tea I put Black Boy into his stable for the night for we were having early frosts already – and did his food in the outhouse and fed him.

Then I heard Mummy calling.

'Jill, are you never coming? What are you doing? The toast is going cold.'

I walked into the cottage and said, 'I've been giving Black Boy his feed and putting him up for the night.'

'Really, dear, if you're going to take so long over one pony, what will you do with two?'

I felt like saying I could as soon see myself winning the open jumping at Olympia as taking any time over Rapide, but I prudently didn't.

'I'm surprised,' said Mummy, 'that you haven't mentioned one thing, where you're going to put Rapide. There obviously isn't room in the stable.'

'Oh, I'm going to board him at the riding school,' I said.

'At Mrs. Darcy's? But, Jill, I'd planned to build you two loose boxes for a Christmas present.'

'You needn't bother,' I said. 'Thanks all the same, Mummy, but it's silly to spend such a lot of money when he can perfectly well live at the riding school. Lots of children keep their ponies there. And Mrs. Darcy won't charge me anything because she can use Rapide for the school.'

Mummy looked at me anxiously. She had been thinking all day that I was going mad, but I took no notice and heated up my toast in the oven and put loads of jam on it, and then sat with my feet up on the fender eating it.

We never mentioned Rapide again that evening, nor the next day which was Sunday. Mummy looked at me in a puzzled way once or twice, but she had something to take her mind off me as she had just begun a new book – I told you in my previous books that Mummy wrote stories about rather whimsical children such as, I think, never were on land or sea – and when she begins a new book she is usually not quite with us, or as Mrs. Crosby (N.R.T.B.) says, 'away with the birds'. So she didn't ask me any awkward questions.

On Sunday morning Mrs. Crosby came to cook our hot lunch while Mummy and I went to church, and in the afternoon I saddled Black Boy and went off by myself for a lovely long ride.

It was a beautiful September day, crisp and sunny, and the leaves were beginning to turn yellow and gleamed in the sun like little gold coins. The sky was very blue and the fields and hills were lovely colours. I rode right across Neshbury Common and through what we call the Top Woods where there are grassy or pine-needle rides all the way, and then we crossed the main road and went along the bridle path round the old golf course and back down Milden Hill which is long and has a grass border which Black Boy loves. I think all roads ought to have grass borders for horses and when I get into Parliament I am going to see about it. I sometimes have visions of getting into Parliament and as long as I can combine it with being an M.F.H. and matron of a big jolly orphanage at the same time, I don't see why I shouldn't.

We were out on this ride for about three hours and both Black Boy and I were dead tired when we got home, with that lovely fresh-air tiredness that knows it is soon going to wallow in warmth and food. Though I was aching all over when I got in I rubbed my pony down, fed him and put him up for the night. He looked beautifully contented and happy when I kissed him good night (I expect you think that is a soppy thing to do but I don't care) and he gave me a soulful look and his jaws just went round and round blissfully on his oats in a rather American manner. He looked sweet. I wouldn't even let myself think of Rapide.

I tiptoed into the cottage by the back door. The kitchen fire was nearly out and from the sitting-room came the weary, dreary rattle of Mummy's typewriter. She had been at it ever since lunch.

I crept upstairs, filled the bath, and got in. It was lovely. Then I suddenly had the feeling I had been rather a beast to Mummy. I expect you have all had that feeling at times but with me it always comes at the most inconvenient moments like now when I didn't want to get out of that nice hot bath. But conscience shoved me out all right. I got dressed and went downstairs. Rattle, rattle, rattle, went Mummy's typewriter, earning our bread and butter and other things. The fire was out, but I boiled the kettle on the hot-plate and made some tea and cut some bread and butter so thinly that you could have read *Horse and Hound* through it, and rummaged about and found the strawberry jam which Mrs. Crosby hides because it is supposed by her to be too good to be eaten all at once by me, and I put all these things on a tray with the nicest cups and saucers and took it into the sitting-room. It was past six o'clock.

Mummy looked at me with the air of one slowly floating down to earth.

'Oh, Jill, you are a dear to think of tea. Somehow when I'm working the time flies and I never think of meals at all. I don't know what I'd do if you didn't look after me.'

'And I don't know what I'd do if you didn't work so hard for us both,' I said. By now my feeling of beastliness had fled. We ate our tea, and I said, 'Do tell me what the new book is going to be about, Mummy.'

'Well, it's going to be called *Angeline, the Fairy Child*,' she said enthusiastically, 'and it's about –'

She went on telling me what it was about between bites of bread and butter and strawberry jam, and I wished I could be more literary and appreciate Mummy's up-in-the-clouds stories as some children must have done or they wouldn't have bought them.

'I'm not too keen on the name Angeline,' I said. 'It's a bit corny, Mummy.'

'I think it's a lovely name,' said Mummy, and we argued happily for a bit. But we never mentioned Rapide.

Next morning as soon as I got into the form room my friend Ann Derry rushed up to me.

'Did you buy it?' she cried excitedly. 'The pony, I mean.'

'Yes I did,' I said, putting down my case and re- membering that I had left my history note-book on the top of the corn-bin in the outhouse.

'What's he like? Do tell me!'

'He's all right,' I said. It was just as if something was clamping me down when I tried to talk about Rapide.

'Well, if you don't want to tell me you needn't,' said Ann rather huffily.

'I've told you,' I said. 'He's all right. He's quite a good pony and he can jump. There isn't anything else to say, is there?'

She just stared at me, because of course I am usually a person who has a great deal to say about everything. I thought gloomily that ever since Rapide had come into my life all my nearest and dearest had begun to think I was bats. Perhaps I would be bats before I had finished with Rapide.

By break-time it was all over the form that I had bought a show jumper. Everybody was interested because most of them rode, and I had been meeting them in the show ring for the last two summers.

'So you've bought a new pony, for jumping?' said Susan Pyke as we ate our biscuits. 'I *shall* have to pull my socks up!'

I could have pointed out that I had beaten her in most events only that very summer but I felt too low to bother.

'What's he like? What's he called?' everybody was

shouting at me. I'm sure they thought I had some sinister reason for being dumb about Rapide because it would never occur to them that anybody could be so mad as to buy a pony she didn't like.

I felt miserable by the time I went home that afternoon, and after tea I couldn't bear it any longer so I went over to see Martin Lowe who is the grandest person and taught me to ride, though he has to sit in a wheel-chair all the time because he lost the use of his legs when he was in the R.A.F. in the war.

I always liked going to the Lowes'. I liked their house which was big and old-fashioned and countryfied and I liked all the whips and photographs of horses and the trophies which were hung up on the walls, and the piles of *Horse and Hound* in places where most houses have dreary magazines about knitting and fashions, and the wonderful stables at the back, and the way their groom hissed – all grooms hiss but the Lowes' groom was the world's champion hisser – and the huge paddock, and the sort of meals the Lowes had, and their cook who could make peppermint creams, and the general horsiness of everything. The only thing I didn't like was the way Mrs. Lowe always treated me as if I were six, only Martin said she did that to him too.

Martin was writing in the dining-room with the window open as I rode up on Black Boy, and he shouted, 'Come in! You haven't been to see us for ages. I expect you're dying to tell me about the new pony. You did buy him, I suppose?'

I dismounted in a nonchalant sort of way – at least

I hoped it looked like that – and tethered my pony.
Then I went into the house.

'How's things?' said Martin.

'All right,' I said.

'*Now* what's the matter?'

'Nothing,' I said.

He picked up his pen and just went on writing, as
much as to say, 'If that's all you're going to tell me,
why did you come?'

I knew I was being silly and rude, so in a minute
out it all came.

'Oh Martin,' I said, 'he's awful. And he loathes
me with a deadly loathing.'

(I got that bit out of an old-fashioned novel. I do think that people in the olden days used to say things in a much more exciting way than we do now.)

Martin put his pen down and asked calmly, 'What on earth did you buy him for?'

I poured out the story of the dismal visit to the Penberthys', and not wanting to disappoint Mummy who liked Mrs. Penberthy so much, and about Rapide having turned against me from the very start and how he jumped a clear round for Joan Penberthy and wouldn't do a thing for me.

'So I bought him,' I said, 'just to show him that I wouldn't be beaten.'

'Well, that's one reason for buying a pony,' said Martin.

'I know it's batty,' I said. 'Oh, do please understand.'

'But it isn't at all batty,' he said. 'Friends of mine have done it before and it has all turned out extremely well. It's a perfectly good reason for buying a horse and shows you have the right spirit. Good luck to you.'

'Oh Martin, I'm so relieved I could pass out!' I said. 'Promise me you'll never let Mummy know how I feel about Rapide. She thinks he's wonderful.'

'I shan't let a single hair of the cat out of the bag,' he said. 'You say this pony is actually a good pony and can jump?'

'Oh yes, he's been well schooled. I saw him do six jumps that were the kind you get in the under-sixteens.

He's won masses of prizes for Joan Penberthy. But he's got the weirdest action. He canters up to the jump, then checks and stops dead. Then he pops up his fore-legs, sort of bucks up his middle, pops up his hind-legs and he's over. I can't think how he does it. I did so hope I'd get a soaring kind of jumper.'

'You don't think he's a mean-spirited pony?'

'No-oo,' I said slowly. 'It was just the way he looked at *me*, as much as to say, Who is this lower-than-worms creature? And I felt such a fool when he wouldn't try to jump for me. Mummy thought I was letting her down and the Penberthys thought I'd never tried to jump before. That was when I decided to buy Rapide. Rapide! Isn't it a silly name? He looks more like the Rocking-Horse Fly.'

'Well, I shall look on with interest to see what you make of him,' said Martin. 'After all, you can always sell him again.'

This thought, which hadn't occurred to me, cheered me up so much that I felt quite happy, and we went out to look at the horses and ate some peppermint creams in the kitchen.

3 - Rapide is here

WEDNESDAY dawned and it was the Day of Doom on which Rapide was going to arrive. We had arranged for Wednesday as it was my half-holiday and I could go and fetch him from the station. He was due to arrive at Chatton at 2.15, so after lunch I changed into my riding things and picked up a halter. I wondered for a minute whether I should ride Black Boy and lead Rapide, but I decided to walk. It was silly of me but I didn't want Rapide to give my nice pony any of his black looks.

I got down to the station and went into the office. The clerk took me to a siding. Rapide had not only arrived but somebody had kindly taken him out of the horse-box and tethered him to some railings, and there he stood giving little shivers and casting dirty looks at everybody and everything in sight.

'Now that's what I call a nice pony,' said the clerk.

I just said 'Hmph,' or something like that.

'What colour would you call him?' asked the clerk.

'He's a bay,' I said.

'I never could understand these horse colours,' said

the clerk. 'I mean, you always call a white horse a grey, don't you?'

'Oh yes,' I said. 'And bay means a reddish brown, and then there's chestnut which is dark brown and roan which is light brown, but you sometimes hear people talk about light chestnut and dark chestnut and light bay and dark bay and light roan and dark roan, which is a bit vague and unhorsemanlike, I think. And then of course there's piebald which is black and white and skewbald which is any other colour and white.'

'You don't say!' said the clerk, unconscious that I was prattling on to put off the evil moment when I should have to tell Rapide I was here.

'Have you come for the pony?' said a porter coming up. 'Would he like a drink after his journey?'

He fetched a bucket of water and Rapide condescended to bury his nose in it and drink, making disgusting noises. I was ashamed of him, but the clerk and porter went on saying what a nice pony he was, in spite of the way he kept looking at them as if they were earwigs.

He had on an old, knotted halter which doubtless Joan Penberthy had thought good enough for him to travel in, so I took it off and threw it away and put on my nice white one. His skin shivered everywhere I touched it, and when his enormous eye was close to me it looked more disdainful and nasty than ever.

'Come on, you!' I said.

'I've seen you riding in the shows,' said the porter. 'You're good, aren't you?'

'Oh not very,' I said. 'Heaps of people are better than me. I've improved though since I had lessons at the riding school.'

'Which one is that?' he asked.

'Mrs. Darcy's at Ring Hill.'

'They say she's going out of fashion,' he said. 'All the kids nowadays are going to this new place, Lime Farm.'

'Then they're silly,' I said. 'Mrs. Darcy is much the best teacher in this county.'

I had got Rapide moving by now. He came along not exactly willingly but sort of unprotestingly, like a French aristo being dragged through the streets of Paris by the mob.

'Well, I expect you'll be winning the open jumping now, ha-ha!' said the porter, which I didn't think was very funny.

I got Rapide home and Mummy was standing at the cottage gate to greet us, looking very excited, as we had talked so much about me having a new pony.

'He doesn't look any the worse for his journey, does he?' she said. 'He is a lovely colour.'

She held a carrot she had saved – and scrubbed – for this moment. Rapide sniffed at it, then turned his head away and looked bored stiff.

'Good gracious!' said Mummy. 'Doesn't he like carrot?'

'I suppose what he really likes is a dessert apple carefully peeled with a silver knife,' I said sarkily.

'What are you going to do with him now?'

'I'm going to put him in the orchard to have a rest after his journey – Black Boy's in the stable – and after tea I'll take him up to Mrs. Darcy's.'

I shoved Rapide into the orchard. He took a long lazy look round and decided it wasn't bad, then began to crop grass.

Mummy came out and began to feed her hens. I can't say I am very taken with the hen as an animal, it has such a soulless expression on its face, but Mummy has such a beautiful nature that she actually likes hens for themselves alone and gives them names like Bonnie and Blossom, and *thanks* them for laying eggs. One year Mummy bought three cockerels to fatten up for the table. We called them Winken, Blinken and Nod. On Christmas Eve she got a man

T–B

to come round and kill one of them for our Christmas dinner and we all went into the yard to choose which should be killed. They all three looked very fat and eatable and quite unconscious that the day of doom had arrived for them, which was rather sad.

Mummy said, 'Well, it can't be Winken because yesterday he took a bit of corn out of my fingers and it was so trusting of him. And it can't be Blinken because I love the way he puts his head on one side. It reminds me of a dog I had when I was small. And it can't be Nod because he looks so comical when he scratches I'm sure he has a sense of humour.'

The man said, 'Well, make up your mind, madam,' and Mummy said, 'No, not one of them shall be killed, they're all personal friends.'

So the man went away and I'm sure he thought we were far from sane, and Mummy and I cheerfully ate sausages and bread sauce for Christmas dinner. This just shows you what Mummy thinks of even such mere things as hens, and the only one we ever ate was one called Mrs. Hitler who pecked at the others and had a mean and unworthy nature.

I went to the little outhouse which I sometimes called the saddle room and sometimes the forage room when I wanted to sound grand, and fetched a few oats for Rapide. He deigned to eat them, not in a nice affectionate pony-ish way at all, but looking at me as if I was trying to poison him.

After tea I saddled Black Boy, and leading Rapide I set off for Mrs. Darcy's riding school and stables at Ring Hill. I always felt grateful to Mrs. Darcy because she was so decent to me when I first got a pony and was such a bad rider, and she also let me work in her stable for a while, where I got a good deal of my present experience. Some people were terrified of her because she was so efficient and everything she said seemed to end in an exclamation mark, and if you did anything ham-handed or quite silly she came down on you like a ton of bricks. But she was awfully nice really and since I had been having regular lessons from her my riding had improved no end, and I had also learned a good deal about that most noble of all creatures, The Horse.

When I turned in at the white gate from which a bridle path ran round the paddock to the yard, Joey, Mrs. Darcy's stable-man, caught sight of me and I saw him run to find her.

She came to meet me and cried, 'Well, well! The new jumper! And a very nice pony too!'

Oh dear, I thought, everybody but me thinks Rapide is a nice pony. Are they all crazy or am I?

I slipped down off Black Boy, and said, 'He came today. Do you think he's all right?'

'Well, he has lovely hocks,' said Mrs. Darcy. 'His rump is higher than his withers.'

'I know,' I said humbly, 'but I think it makes him look like a worn-down steeple-chaser, or even a kangaroo. And don't you think his neck is rather unyielding?'

'Why, what's the matter, Jill?' she said. 'You're talking about your new pony in a very disparaging way. I thought you'd have been wild with enthusiasm.'

Then of course I had to pour it all out again. I felt rather a fool, telling an expert like Mrs. Darcy that I didn't like Rapide and he didn't like me and I had only bought him from sheer cussedness and to save Mummy from being disappointed.

'But the point is, can he jump?' said Mrs. Darcy. 'Surely you wouldn't buy a so-called jumper if he couldn't?'

'Oh yes, he can jump,' I said, 'but you should see him! He looks awful. He jumps from a standstill, all buckled up.'

'My dear idiot,' said Mrs. Darcy, 'you're much too conceited about how you look on a pony. That's what you're thinking of, isn't it? Well, I've seen some of the best show jumpers with the most awful conformation, and there are all types of jumpers and ways of jumping. Now just get along home and leave that pony to me, and mind you're up here tomorrow to groom him because goodness knows he needs it after the train journey and nobody here has the time!'

She laughed gaily and took hold of Rapide's halter, and like magic his whole nature seemed to change and he walked humbly along by her side with the meekest look on his face. I felt frightfully humiliated and began to think that after all I didn't know anything about horses.

When I got home Mummy said, 'Well? Did Rapide settle down nicely with Mrs. Darcy?'

I felt like saying, 'And how!' but Mummy has stopped me using American slang so I just said a feeble, 'Yes, thank you,' and went upstairs to change.

4 - Some people will do anything !

IN the middle of the night I woke up suddenly, and it was just like in detective stories where the great detective suddenly sees the vital clue revealed to him as though by a flash of lightning across the midnight sky. He is then overjoyed, but what was revealed to me didn't overjoy me at all, just the opposite. It was something that the porter had said at the station about Mrs. Darcy, 'They say she's going out of fashion. All the kids nowadays are going to this new place, Lime Farm.'

As I thought this over I went hot and cold, and I knew I couldn't go to sleep any more so I put my dressing-gown on and sat up in bed, nursing my knees and feeling miserable. I daren't put the light on in case Mummy saw the reflection and came in.

I must have been pretty blind, but now a lot of things were clear to me. Angela, Mrs. Darcy's head girl who used to ride her horses in the Hunter Trials and Grade C Jumping, Stackwood who drove the horse-box and looked after the ponies at shows, and other dependable people had gone off to other jobs

and now Mrs. Darcy was doing all the skilled jobs
herself with only the help of Joey – who loved horses
but wasn't very bright so nobody would employ
him – and a girl of fifteen called Wendy Mead who
helped at week-ends and odd times in return for riding
lessons. And when I thought about it still more – and
it hurts like anything thinking in the middle of the
night because you get so hungry – I realized that it
was months since Mrs. Darcy got any new pupils.
And yet lots of new children were learning to ride,
and they were all going to Lime Farm!

Lime Farm belonged to some people called Captain
and Mrs. Drafter and it was a very dashing sort of
place with gallons of new green and white paint
splashed about, and all the horses there had dark
green blankets bound with yellow, and E.D. in the
corner. E.D. were the initials of Captain Drafter. I
don't know what the E. stood for but I expect it was
something revolting like Ebenezer or Eustace. Captain
Drafter was very tall and thin and had a bluish face
with a nose like a setter and hard little eyes like unripe
gooseberries. He rode a jet black hunter that was
supposed to be worth hundreds of pounds, and when
he was hunting he took a flea-bitten grey as his second
horse that was also frightfully valuable and nipped
other people's less wonderful horses, and the Master
had had to speak to him more than once, which I think
is the lowest form of disgrace.

Mrs. Drafter rode side-saddle, which I think was
just to show that she could do it, and used her whip an
awful lot. Ours is a very friendly Hunt and the Master

encourages children to follow on their ponies, and even on bikes and on foot if they haven't ponies, which doesn't shut anybody out just because they are poor and honest, but Mrs. Drafter looked round and said, 'What a rabble'. I looked Rabble up in the dictionary and it said, a disorderly crowd or mob, which was quite untrue and makes one think of the French Revolution and not a lot of nice children who were keen on riding, so I always hated Mrs. Drafter ever after.

All the pupils at Lime Farm Riding School were taught to ride in a very dashing way, which pleased the sort of parents who had loads of money but didn't know much about the noble art of equitation, and Susan Pyke was the star pupil. And it was sad but true that all the new children were going to Lime Farm, and not to Mrs. Darcy's where they would have learned to ride well and have good manners and care for their ponies.

By the time all these Frightful Facts had come to me I was very cold and practically starving. I tried to go to sleep again but I couldn't. It was no use, I had to go downstairs and find something to eat, so I didn't even put my slippers on as they are apt to go slippety-slop, and I sneaked down the stairs on my bare feet so as not to waken Mummy. I didn't even put the light on in the kitchen because the switch makes such a click – isn't it funny how switches click like mad in the night and don't make a sound in the daytime? – and I groped my way to the cupboard where the tin of biscuits is kept, and opened the door and felt my way up to the second shelf. I had just got hold of the edge of the biscuit tin when my dressing-gown sleeve caught something and over it went! The next minute there was a hideous crash, then thud, thud, thud, and the sound of something rolling over the kitchen floor. I put on the light. What I had knocked down was a big pudding basin, right on to the jars of new-made blackberry jelly which Mummy had left to set on the ledge under the cupboard. Four of them had gone over like ninepins, and all across the kitchen floor was a trail of purple jelly which made me wonder how so much could ever have been crammed into only four jars.

Of course by then Mummy was in my midst, so to speak, and she was furious and told me I might at least have had the sense to put the light on before rummaging in the cupboards, and she didn't seem a bit impressed when I told her I had only been trying not to wake her up, so what with that row and worrying about Mrs. Darcy, to say nothing of a sleepless night and Rapide on my hands, I got up next morning feeling really low.

By the time I had fed Black Boy and done all my early morning jobs and had some cocoa and sausages I felt a bit better – because food is very good for sorrow – so I thought I would bike up to Mrs. Darcy's before school and have a look at Rapide.

As I jumped off my bike in the stable yard the sight of two empty loose boxes looking too horribly clean and bare for words reminded me that Mrs. Darcy had been selling ponies instead of buying them. I decided that being a detective was very depressing.

'Hullo, Jill!' she called out, coming towards me with her shirt sleeves rolled up and her arms full of tack she had been cleaning. 'Have you come to see how Rapide is? Well, he's still alive, you'll be glad to hear. Wendy had him out for half an hour before breakfast and she says she thinks he has it in him but is rather unresponsive. She hasn't jumped him, of course.'

Rapide was in the middle of his breakfast. He took his nose out long enough to look at me as if I were a spider he had found in his oats.

I said, 'Good boy!' rather half-heartedly and stroked his nose. He shied, side-stepped into Mrs. Darcy, rebounded towards me and fairly snorted his disgust.

'I'll tell you what,' she said, 'I think there's something funny about those Penberthys of yours. This pony has been ill-treated or I know nothing about horses.'

'Oh no!' I said. 'It couldn't – I mean, he couldn't – they couldn't. They were terribly nice and truly horsy people, and it was only me that seemed all wrong that day, and Joan Penberthy did six clear jumps on him, and he's won her stacks of cups and things.'

'Fish!' said Mrs. Darcy, which was her way of saying, Rot. 'I've got a strong idea that your Joan Penberthy's idea of schooling a pony is to whip him round the jumps until he takes them in sheer terror of being whipped. Is that what they did to you, eh, Rapide?'

'I can't believe it,' I gasped.

'My dear Jill, when you've been in the horse world as long as I have you'll know that there are people who will do *anything*, and then pass themselves off as nice, horsy people – as you call it. Well, you've bought Rapide, and I expect now you'll want to sell him again.'

'Would that be a good thing?' I asked.

'Well, you certainly won't want to bother with him. I'll get rid of him for you, if you like, and then you can find something easier and more to your liking.'

'Who would you sell him to?' I asked.

'I'd probably send him to auction. I don't do that to my own ponies but I haven't any feelings about Rapide. I daresay he'd make a good pony for a tradesman.'

'But what will Mummy say?'

'Oh, I'll put that right,' said Mrs. Darcy kindly. 'I'll tell her I don't think Rapide is suitable for you and that I'll help you to find something better. She won't mind.'

'Oh, thank you very much, Mrs. Darcy,' I said. 'It is kind of you.' I then looked at my watch and said, 'Oh help, it's a quarter to nine. I'll have to pedal like mad to get to school.'

A great weight had rolled off my mind. I was never going to see Rapide again, it was too good to be true.

At break I grabbed hold of Ann Derry and dragged her to a rather sordid part of the school garden where they kept the grass clippings and things that had lost their handles, and there were bits of old bonfire lying about and it was smelly too, but nice and private.

'Listen,' I said, 'it's terribly important. I've been awake for hours in the night. We've got to start a campaign.'

'What's that?' she said densely.

'Like a crusade,' I said, 'only more tough. I mean, the Crusades went on for years and never got anywhere, but Wellington had campaigns and they overthrew Napoleon.'

'Gosh, are you trying to be top in history, or something?' she said.

'No,' I said. 'It's about Mrs. Darcy and the riding school.'

And I told her all about everything I had thought of in the silent watches of the night.

'Yes, it's true,' said Ann. 'There are some new people in our road and they have a Rolls-Royce and a beastly girl called Patience, and her mother came to tea and asked Mummy if I went to Lime Farm Riding School and Mummy said no, to Mrs. Darcy's, and Patience's mother said, "Oh, but they tell me that Lime Farm is *the* place. Patience has started there already." And then Mummy asked me if I was satisfied with Mrs. Darcy's or would I like to change and go to Lime Farm too.'

'Gosh! What did you say?'

'I said that the very fact that Susan Pyke had changed to Lime Farm was enough to put me off it, and Mummy doesn't like the Pykes either so she didn't say any more.'

'Well we've got to do something about it,' I said. 'But the point is, what?'

'We'd better start a club,' said Ann, 'and get some of the decent people like the Heaths and Diana Bush to join. We could call it the B.L.F. Club, Bar Lime Farm, you know.'

Ann was always very good at thinking of names for things.

'I think it sounds a bit rude,' I said. 'It isn't much good starting off by being rude, or our mothers might bar the Club. What about calling it the B.M.D. – Boost Mrs. Darcy.'

'Oh gosh, yes!' said Ann. 'I think that's terrific.'

'Okay,' I said. 'That's enough for now, and the bell's just going. But in Geography you can think like mad about things the B.M.D. can do, and I'll think too. And I'll see you after school.'

After school we hadn't really thought of anything, but we told Diana Bush and the Heaths and they said they would join, so we decided to have a meeting the next day in the dinner hour.

Ann and I biked home together and all of a sudden she said, 'By the way, how's Rapide? Have you had a chance to try him yet?'

'Oh, I'm selling him,' I said. 'Mrs. Darcy's going to send him to auction.'

'What for?' said Ann, nearly falling off her bike but saving herself by a daring dirt-track swerve while an old lady on the pavement said 'Tch-tch-tch.'

So I told her what Mrs. Darcy had said and all the awful revelations about the Penberthys being fiends in human shape and about it being too much trouble to try and do anything with Rapide, and how I was

going to get a really good pony, and was frightfully relieved at the thought that I should never see Rapide any more.

'Well, of all the soulless things I ever heard,' said Ann, 'I call that the utter grimikins.'

'How do you mean?' I said haughtily.

'I mean, you go and drag a poor ill-treated pony away from its horrible owners and take it to a nice place like Mrs. Darcy's and give it the idea that it's going to live there for ever and ever, and just when joy is waking in its down-trodden heart and it thinks that it might even have a shot at being a jolly decent pony in return for people being kind to it, you go and shove it into a beastly auction and it will be bought by a cold-blooded baker with brutal eyes and he'll make it pull about forty times more than it can, and one day it'll fall down on a hill and die. And you talk about loving horses!'

'Oh, don't be silly, Ann,' I said. 'Rapide will probably be bought by a terribly nice greengrocer and he'll be able to turn his head round and eat the dessert apples off the cart.'

But talking about dessert apples gave me a nasty cold feeling down my spine as I remembered how Mummy had offered Rapide a carrot and he had turned his head away. Could it be because nobody had ever kindly offered him anything before in his life, but hit his nose instead? I went colder and colder until I was cold all over. When we got to Ann's road I just said, 'Flog-oh' – which we had got from a radio programme and were saying a lot just then – and hared off home. Mummy was out so I made a cup of cocoa and sat on the kitchen floor and drank it. And I thought and thought and the more I thought the more awful I felt. I wished Ann hadn't said that about Rapide thinking he had got to a good home at last and then having all his hopes dashed to the ground. And of course I didn't really believe about the cold-blooded baker – because bakers can't help being nice when they have such lovely shops full of luscious things to eat – but I had to remember the poor pony I bought in my other book called *A Stable for Jill* from a disgusting man called J. Biggs who sold firewood and was a beast of the first water. And I suppose if there was one J. Biggs there might be others. Perhaps that very J. Biggs was looking for another pony by now and might buy Rapide?

By the time Mummy came in I felt quite weird with thinking so much.

5 - That pony again

AFTER supper I said I was going to Mrs. Darcy's. Mummy said, 'Now look here, Jill, I oughtn't to have to speak to you about all this running off to the riding school. It's a weekday and your lessons ought to come first. You never seem to be thinking of anything but those ponies.'

'But it's important,' I said, 'and I've done my homework. I did it before you came in. Please, Mummy! I'll only be ten minutes.'

So she said I could go but I must be back before dark. I biked along like mad. I seemed to have spent most of the day rushing about.

Everything at the stables was closed up for the night, so I went and knocked on the house door. Mrs. Darcy opened it. She and Zoe were having their supper. Zoe was Mrs. Darcy's niece who stayed with her, and we were rather frightened of her as she had been second in the under-sixteen jumping at Richmond Horse Show.

'Have you sold Rapide yet?' I blurted out.

'Yes,' said Mrs. Darcy, and my heart sank. 'At least I've sent him over to Bidworth. There's a horse sale there tomorrow, mostly working horses. You ought to get a good price for Rapide.'

'Could we get him back?' I said. 'I've decided I don't want to sell him.'

'But you said you did,' said Zoe.

'Well, would you?' I said. 'You may think I don't know my own mind, but such utterly soulless people buy horses, and just when Rapide thought he was getting a good home –'

'I see just what you mean,' said Zoe, and I felt grateful to her, and wasn't frightened of her any more. 'I couldn't sell a pony I'd had anything to do with unless I knew the home it was going to.'

Mrs. Darcy smiled all over her face.

'Are you prepared to take a lot of trouble with Rapide?' she said, looking at me. 'Or will you be sorry in a day or two that you went all soft about him?'

'If he's worth taking trouble with, I'll take it,' I said.

'I think he is and so does Zoe.'

'Oh, please get him back,' I said, feeling awful at the thought of what poor Rapide must be feeling like now, all among strangers and perhaps tied up to a ring in a dirty wall in a large, empty hall, which is the kind of place where they sell horses.

'I'll ring up at once,' said Mrs. Darcy, 'and tell them to withdraw Rapide, and Joey can go over in the morning and fetch him back.'

I hovered about while she telephoned, standing first on one leg and then on the other, and at last Mrs. Darcy came and said it was all settled, I had got

Rapide again. I said 'thank you' about nine times, and Mrs. Darcy started telling Zoe about Chatton Show where I had won a few events, and I looked at the photos of hunters on the wall and wondered what Mrs. Darcy would think if she knew about the B.M.D.

Next day at school I said to Ann, 'I do think you're a wash-out. You've made me take Rapide back, and now if he gets me twenty-four faults it'll be your fault.'

She just said, 'I thought your Better Self would Triumph,' which I recognized as being out of a book which our domestic science mistress read to us while we did darning.

In the dinner hour it rained, so we got the members of the Club together and went and sat by the radiator in the gym.

I started off the meeting by saying, 'Some of you ought to have thought of something by now.'

Actually I felt a bit guilty as, with all that Rapide business, I hadn't had time to think of a thing myself.

'Daddy was telling us last night,' said Val Heath, 'about when he was abroad somewhere – I don't exactly remember where – but they were boosting something up – only I forget what it was but it doesn't matter because it was *something* – and they started off with about an hour of fireworks and people came from miles around to see what it was, and then they sent up rockets and then flares and whatever it was they were trying to boost was written in green and red letters all over the sky. It must have been whizzo.'

'Well, that would cost a million pounds,' I said witheringly. 'Doesn't anybody know anything cheap?'

'If it's carrying banners and marching,' said Jackie Heath, 'I'm jolly well not going to.'

'I take a dim view of that too,' said Diana Bush. 'I asked my mother about it last night and she says the only thing we can do is to display such good horse-manship and good manners that everybody will see how much better taught we are than the Lime Farm crowd.'

'But that'll take such a long time,' said Ann. 'I mean, we can't wait until next summer's events to boost Mrs. Darcy. She may not have any riding school left by then – except us.'

'There's the Hunter Trials,' said Diana.

'That's mostly for grown-ups, and two events for under-sixteens.'

'I think in a way Diana's right,' I said, 'and we've simply got to do well at the Hunter Trials. But we must do something else too. There are a lot of new girls in the school and they're sure to get keen on riding soon with hearing us talk about nothing else, and we've got to make sure that they'll go to Mrs. Darcy and not to those Drafter people.'

'I know!' shouted Ann. 'Let's write a letter to all the new girls and tell them all about it and ask them to go to Mrs. Darcy's and not Lime Farm. Like an advertisement.'

'Oh yes,' said Val Heath, 'and I could paint a skull at the top. I can paint the most marvellous skulls.'

'I think that's silly,' said Diana. 'We ought to put at the top, "In the cause of Good Riding," or some-thing sensible like that.'

'I've got it!' I fairly yelled. 'Not a letter, just an advertisement. "For good riding's sake go to Mrs. Darcy's." And we could do it on postcards.'

'Oughtn't we to say something about how awful the riding is at Lime Farm?' said Jackie.

'They could send you to prison if you did,' said Diana. 'It's called libel, or something.'

'There are about twenty new girls,' I said, 'and there are five of us, so that means doing four postcards each and we can put them in their desks.'

'I'll get the postcards,' said Ann. 'Daddy has masses of them in his study, I'll bring some tomorrow.'

We were all excited about doing the postcards, and next day Ann brought them to school and we all took four home to do. I whizzed through my homework and then lettered the postcards in pencil and went over the outlines in Indian ink and then round the capital letters in red paint. They looked terrific and I laid them out on the kitchen table to dry. FOR GOOD RIDING'S SAKE GO TO MRS. DARCY'S done four times over made me feel as if something was really happening. Mummy was thinking about something else, as she often is, and didn't even notice what I was doing. She just wandered by and murmured, 'Making Christmas cards, dear?'

Next morning at break we collected our buns and met on the net-ball court. Everybody had done their postcards. Ann had done each one of her four in a different colour, red, blue, green and purple, and Val Heath had painted a little skull on hers but she said it was just her signature and didn't mean anything, and

Diana had forgotten the word 'sake' so her cards said, FOR GOOD RIDING'S GO TO MRS. DARCY'S which made sense, so we didn't bother to have them done again.

We soon found out who the new girls were and which forms they were in and where they sat, so in the dinner hour we nipped round the form rooms and did the deed, and that was that.

As we came out of school in the afternoon Ann said, 'I wonder if Mrs. Darcy has got Rapide back? I expect she has by now. Couldn't we go and have a look at him? I'm dying to see him.'

I didn't feel at all enthusiastic, in fact all day I had been trying to forget Rapide, so I muttered something about going straight home.

'I think you're a horrid meanie if you don't let me go with you,' said Ann.

'And us too!' shouted Diana, Val, and Jackie who had overheard all Ann's tactless remarks. 'We took you to see our new ponies.'

I tried to mumble something about Mummy wondering where I was, but it didn't work because they all pointed out that we'd be passing the cottage in any case and they'd gladly wait while I went in and explained. So we set off, and on the way I told them that Rapide was really a cross between a Gorgon and a rocking-horse and had been wished on me by an evil fairy and that all who gazed on him were doomed to frightful mishaps.

'What a scream!' said Diana. 'What sort of mishaps?'

'For you,' I said, 'it will be losing your stirrup

irons. Every time you go out you'll never for a minute be able to keep your feet in your stirrup irons. Jackie's pony will run out of every competition and Val's will bite the judge, not just once but every time.'

'What's going to happen to me,' said Ann, 'if I gaze on Rapide.'

'I'll tell you,' I said. 'Your mother will send you to Lime Farm to learn to ride, and Captain Drafter will take you out on a leading rein with the tiny tots.'

They all said I was crackers.

We stopped at the cottage and I went in. Mummy was in the sitting-room, typing. I went and hovered over her a bit, then I said, 'You do type well, but it wastes your time to have to do all that copying. I could soon learn to type and do it for you.'

'That's an idea,' she said, 'but I'm busy now so don't bother me, there's a good girl.'

'I'm rather in the mood for learning to type now, this minute,' I said.

'And I'm rather in the mood to get on with this by myself,' said Mummy. 'Thanks very much all the same. Now do push off.'

'Don't you want me to make the tea?' I said.

'It's too early for tea,' said my callous mother with a complete lack of intuition. 'Let's wait till about half-past five.'

'Isn't there anything you want me to do?' I said. 'I mean, I'm quite free at the moment.'

'You've already made me type the same line twice,' said Mummy. 'And what are those girls doing out-side? Good gracious!'

My friends' faces were pressed against the window-pane, looking in in a very sinister way.

'All is lost!' I said dramatically, but it was wasted because Mummy just said vaguely, 'Yes, you can go out and play with them if that's what you're worrying about. Don't be late back.'

'Play!' I said bitterly.

I couldn't do a thing about it, so I went out and said, 'It's all very inconvenient,' and got on my bike in what is called in some books High Dudgeon. (I once looked this up in the Dic. and there isn't any Low Dudgeon, it's always High.)

'But your mother said you could come,' said Val, who was a bit dim. 'We heard her through the window.'

When we got up to Mrs. Darcy's all was perfect peace. Zoe was cantering a pony round the paddock.

'Where will Rapide be?' said Ann.

'Probably sitting by the fire reading the *Eagle*,' I said with terrific sarcasm.

'I don't think that's a bit funny,' said Diana. 'He's more likely to be lying at the point of death in his stall because his ghastly experiences at the sale have broken his heart.'

'Well, Ann shouldn't say such obvious things,' I said crossly. ' "Where will Rapide be?" Where are ponies usually kept at a stable?'

I pushed open the gate and we all streamed in, then I let it clang to again and we walked up the paddock. Zoe recognized us and came cantering up.

'Hullo,' she said. 'I thought you'd want to see him.

He looks all right, doesn't he?'

She patted her mount's neck. I nearly fell over backwards.

It was Rapide.

When I became conscious again, which was about two minutes later, I heard Ann say, 'I think he's sweet!'

'Oh Zoe, let me try him,' said Diana.

'And then us,' said Val.

'I think he's had enough for today,' said Zoe. 'He's had a long journey back from town, but when he arrived back here he looked round him in a most satisfied way. I rubbed him down and gave him a feed and he ate oats out of my hand. So after he'd had a rest I saddled him and we've had half an hour round the paddock and we've both enjoyed it, haven't we, Rapide?'

Rapide looked at Zoe as much as to say, 'I think you're all right, but defend me from these others.'

'I can't see anything the matter with him,' said Jackie. 'When we were coming along and I saw you in the paddock, Zoe, I thought, what a jolly nice pony. I thought he lifted his feet beautifully. Didn't I say to you, Val, doesn't that pony Zoe's on lift his feet beautifully?'

'Did you?' said Val. 'I don't remember. But I don't think he's a bit like a Gorgon or a rocking-horse either.'

'Is that what Jill told you he was like?' said Zoe. 'She's crackers.'

'It's only me that he doesn't like,' I said.

'Come on, Jill,' said Zoe. 'Get up on him now while's he's in the mood.'

'Not likely,' I said. 'Not in front of all you people, and you said he'd had enough.'

'Well, give him a kind word,' said Zoe, 'for pity's sake.'

'Hullo, Rapide,' I said, cautiously touching his nose. 'So you're back?'

He stepped back hastily into Ann, who sat down looking very surprised. Then he tossed his head about and rolled his eyes at Zoe as much as to say, Take me out of this.

'No go,' said Zoe. 'He's had enough. Come on, let's put him in his stall.'

So rather reluctantly – at least I was reluctant and the others seemed to enjoy it – we went and put Rapide into his stall, and while Zoe unsaddled him Jackie gave him a good hug and he blew at her in a most friendly way.

'Look, he simply adores me,' said Jackie. 'Don't you, darling?'

'I wonder why he doesn't like Jill?' said Ann. 'Perhaps she reminds him of the Penberthy girl.'

'Well, of all the insults!' I said. 'Joan Penberthy was a complete hag.'

'There may be something in what Ann says,' said Zoe. 'It is possible that Rapide associates you with the place he hated. After all, you rode him down there didn't you? You'll have to be awfully kind to him, to make up. I don't think you've been particularly nice to him yet.'

I went rather red, and then somehow we all got away, but I remembered what Zoe had said, and next morning I went up there early by myself, and I fed Rapide and made as much fuss of him as he'd let me. All of a sudden I felt terribly sorry for him, and when you feel really and truly sorry for a person or a horse they seem to know it and a thing called a Bond of Sympathy is Forged. I don't say that the Bond of Sympathy between me and Rapide was very hot all at once, but it began to be there. And that was Something.

6 - The day of the meet

NEXT morning at school we all got it in the neck. As soon as we got back to our form-room after prayers Miss Fox, our form-mistress, said, 'Who is responsible for this unappetizing and illiterate concoction?' – she talks like that – and she held up one of the handwritten slips that we had put in the new girls' desks. It wasn't even one of the better ones either, it was one of the bad ones that Diana had done which said, FOR GOOD RIDING'S GO TO MRS. DARCY'S.

We all looked at each other, and then Ann, Diana, Val, Jackie, and I got up simultaneously and said, 'Me.'

Of course Miss Fox being the English mistress and mad on grammar we couldn't have said anything worse if we'd tried.

I needn't go into details because all my readers who have been in a similar situation will be able to imagine them, but the result was that we all had to stay in that afternoon after school and write out one hundred times a frightfully untrue statement which made our blood boil, namely, THERE ARE MORE IMPORTANT THINGS IN LIFE THAN HORSES.

After I had written this out about twenty-two times I found that I was tapping it out with my feet. (You try it, it's rather fun.) I think Miss Fox must have had what they call a sense of rhythm without knowing it.

Then I found it was even more fun to do it like a five finger exercise.

Anyway, when we eventually got out of prison aching from head to foot, Ann said modestly, 'It was you tapping on the desk, Jill, that gave me an idea and I've written a poem.'

It was such a nice poem that I've put it down here so that you can all see it. I think it ought to be in all poetry books.

LIFE by ANN DERRY

There are more important things in life than horses,
  At least that's what Miss Fox would have us know,
She never went for rides on autumn mornings,
  Or felt the thrill of riding's lovely glow.

There are more important things in life than horses,
  But if your pony loves you, you don't care.
They can keep the things they seem to think important
  And when they dish them out I shan't be there.

There are more important things in life than horses,
  There are more important things in life than food,
But somehow when I'm eating or I'm riding
  There's nothing else in life seems half so good.

You may think the last verse is a bit hoggish, but if you're an honest person you'll have to admit that it's true. I copied this poem out and sent it to my pen-friend in America. My pen-friend in America is the daughter of some people that Mummy stayed with at Philadelphia, and she is awfully nice, though Mummy says my duty is not to give her a misleading idea of English life. I don't know why Mummy should think

I would. I just tell Louise my adventures and she tells me hers, and hers are much more exciting – she was once chased by a bison in a national park – while mine, as you will have gathered from my books, are dull in comparison.

I am sorry to say that after the episode of being kept in to write lines for putting notices on behalf of the Boost Mrs. Darcy Club in the new girls' desks, the Club seemed to lapse a bit. The reason was that we were all being rather restrained at home and at school in case any tactless behaviour of ours suggested to our parents that it might be a good idea to stop us from attending the crack meet of the season which was being held at the end of November. I don't want to raise your hopes by pretending that we were expecting to attend the meet as part of the field because we were far from being members of the Hunt, and children were not allowed to follow at the crack meet in any case, but I and my friend Ann are great believers in being on the spot, because you never know. I once read a book in which a girl of fourteen dressed in her riding clothes went to watch a crack meet, and the Master happened to have a spare horse he wanted ridden, and he said, 'Here, girl, you look as though you could ride, what about hunting Hector for me?' And the girl never turned a hair but vaulted lightly upon Hector's seventeen-hands-high saddle and led the field (you know those hunting stories where everybody goes round by the bridge except the heroine who clears the awful ditch with feet to spare) and finally got the brush.

When I was twelve I might have believed this sort of

thing, and though now I believe it couldn't possibly happen – still, as I said before, you never know.

The night before the meet I went to stay at Ann's house so that we could have the fun of grooming the ponies together next morning. I don't know about fun, as it was the blackest, coldest morning I ever remember, and as we groomed Black Boy and George – who was the new pony Ann got when her old pony Seraphine was handed down to her little sister – our teeth played the castanets in a very Spanish way. It was only six o'clock and we started singing *Oh What a Beautiful Morning* to cheer ourselves up, and Mrs. Derry, who is the world's fussiest mother, put her head out of the bedroom window and called, 'Oh girls, it's much too cold for you, do go back to bed,' which shows you the depths unhorsy people can fall to.

It was rather nice to get our frozen hands into hot water and soapflakes when we washed the tails, but we funked bandaging and plaiting, it was too jolly cold, anyway we weren't actually hunting. Then we fed the ponies and I carried back the bucket to the Derrys' spotless kitchen, and of course I tripped in avoiding a sort of mat thing that was just inside the door (it was so spotless and pure that I couldn't realize it was for such a squalid purpose as wiping the feet on) and went headlong into the kitchen with the bucket going in one direction and the very dirty and soapy contents in the other. I expect you, dear reader, are the sort of person who would have remembered to empty the bucket outside, but I regret I am not like that. Ann came in with the saddles and things and I cleaned up the floor to a certain extent, while she put the kettle on with one hand to make tea and with the other hand began to shake up the metal polish for cleaning our tack. At first the polish wouldn't come, and then it arrived in a gush all over the table, and at that point the Derrys' housekeeper came in and told us that girls of our age with no more sense than we had ought to be in a Home, and take those great ugly saddles out of her kitchen. We daren't say we had come in just for warmth, so we crawled out again into the cheerless dawn and got on with the job of doing the saddles and the leathers and all the metal bits.

Eventually we were ready. We had done our best to look very nice indeed so that if any casual observer happened to say, 'How neat you two girls look,' we should be able to reply that we represented Mrs. Darcy's equitation establishment. We didn't really suppose that anybody would, but again you never know. Our jodhs and coats were speckless and we had new shirts and very well-tied ties and brushed hats and neat hair and what the books call irreproachable gloves and boots. We didn't expect to stay like that for long, but had hopes.

It turned out to be quite a pleasant day for November and we rode off slowly to the *Grinning Mouse* which was where the meet was to be. We saw other people on the way, and presently there was an important sort of clatter and we were overtaken by Susan Pyke and her father mounted on magnificent thoroughbreds. Susan was a member of the Hunt now – her father had given it to her for a birthday present – and she never let anybody forget it. She looked terrific in her black and white, and the gloss on her boots made you blink, but as usual she was riding a horse too big for her, it was her weakness.

'Hullo,' she said in a friendly let's-encourage-the-tiny-tots way, 'going to watch the meet? You'd better hurry. You'll never get there if you jog along like that, you know.'

'Thank you,' said Ann. 'We're not fond of arriving in a lather.'

'Nice little ponies!' said Susan, looking at Black Boy's ears, and my blood boiled as she knew perfectly well that my pony had whacked hers hollow in loads of events when we were both in the under-fourteen classes.

She then used her crop in a very dashing way to go forward and catch up her father, and gave an inelegant lurch and lost one stirrup-iron. Ann and I couldn't help giggling.

The meet as I told you was a crack one, and there were a number of distinguished visitors including Lord and Lady Prance whose pictures you often seen in the *Queen*, if you are the sort of person who goes to the dentist's frequently. The scene outside the *Grinning Mouse* was most exciting and the horses and riders looked wonderful. We hovered on the outskirts with a lot of other people of our age, and when the Master came by we all said good morning and he lifted his cap and smiled at us very gallantly, only nothing book-like happened. I mean, he didn't stop and say how smart we looked and where did we learn to ride,

or ask us if we'd like to hunt on a spare horse he happened to have handy. This was disappointing, but so like Life.

When the Hunt moved off we went along the lane to a place where we could see them draw the first covert. Then the hounds streamed away into the distance with the riders after them, the musical cries and thunder of hoofs died on the still November air, and that was that.

We hadn't done, of course. We followed at a respectful distance, and I must say without seeming to boast that both Black Boy and George jumped marvellously and we even overtook some of the laggards and had to hang back so as not to look as if we were in the field.

There was a check in the middle of an open sixty-acre field and we had a splendid view of the Hunt eating its lunches, so we ate ours and then they were off again – hounds having started another fox out of what we call Mucky Pup Spinney – and this time they streamed away from sight and we followed rather laboriously but lost them and took a wrong turning down a long lane that ended at a farm.

The farmer's wife came out and said, 'Be off with you!' which we thought very unfriendly of her as we hadn't done any harm, so we rode down the long lane again and got back to where we started.

By now presumably the Hunt was miles away and our ponies were blowing.

'What now?' said Ann. 'Are we going in search?'

'There doesn't seem to be anybody to ask,' I said.

Just at that minute a rustic swain appeared with a load of turnips, and when we asked him if he had seen anything of the Hunt he said he had seen them going full cry towards Ritchwell Forest ages ago and they would be miles away by now.

It was disappointing, and as we didn't quite know where we were ourselves we asked him, and found we were miles from home. It was nearly three o'clock, so when he obligingly pointed out a short cut we thanked him and galloped down a long steep field, only to find that we had to toil up an even longer, steeper field at the other side which our tired ponies didn't enjoy one bit. We decided that we should have asked for the nearest road and stuck to it, but one hates to do obvious sensible things like that on a hunting day.

Eventually we found ourselves on a common full of rabbit holes, in fact there were so many that we dismounted and led the ponies.

'Listen, can you hear anything?' said Ann.

'What sort of thing?' I said.

'A dog whining,' she said.

'Yes I can!' I cried. 'It's quite near, but there's no dog.'

'Gosh!' shrieked Ann. 'It's in a rabbit hole. I bet it's a hound. Come on, let's search.'

We crawled about on the ground for a bit, and anybody who had seen us would have thought we were raving, but there was no one to see us, and as twilight fell we at last located the very hole from which the faint whimperings came.

'He's down there,' I said. 'Poor old thing. If he'd only stop scratching and not use his strength up. I say, what a good thing we came along.'

'We're not much good without a spade,' said Ann. 'You wait there and I'll go and find the nearest farm and borrow one.'

To make a long story short she was gone half an hour, but at last she came back with a fork.

'You might have brought a man,' I said. 'This ground'll be frightful to dig. And the dog's gone quiet, I expect he's suffocated.'

'There wasn't a man,' said Ann. 'There was only a woman and she wasn't at all pleasant either.'

For the next twenty minutes we nearly broke our backs wielding the fork. It was almost dark, I lost my hat and never found it again, and our gloves which we kept on to save our hands were in ribbons. At long last we got through to the burrow, and Ann lay flat and shoved her arm down it, struggled a bit and cried out, 'I've got him.'

Between us we managed to drag out a young hound, absolutely plastered with earth and quite exhausted.

'That's what you get,' I told him, 'for leaving the hunt and going off after rabbits.'

We were nearly as exhausted as the hound and a mass of blisters and aching bones, so we sat down and had a rather cold, damp rest and then, quite forgetting to return the fork to the farm, we trudged wearily off, leading the ponies, and the hound on a sort of halter and lead made out of the lucky piece of string I always carry in my pocket for emergencies. This was an emergency all right.

Soon we struck a main road and found a signpost and made for home, riding, and taking it in turns to hold Ranter's string. We called him Ranter because of John Peel. We had to call him something.

It was a slow ride and we were starving, besides wondering what sort of welcome we were going to get from our loving parents who had told us on no account to be out after five. It was already past six.

'I feel this is the beginning of something wonderful,' said Ann.

'Such as?' I asked sarkily.

'Well, you know this might easily prove to be the Master's favourite hound. Or it might be Lord and Lady Prance's favourite hound. Anyway, we shall be invited to Moss Hall and given a banquet, and gold tie-pins with foxes' heads.'

'And we'll tell Lord and Lady Prance about Mrs. Darcy's,' I said, 'and they will send their five daughters there, and Mrs. Darcy will be made for life.'

'Good show!' said Ann.

We decided that we would take the hound straight home to our cottage, and next morning we would get up at six and make ourselves look very tidy and we'd sponge and press our clothes and groom the ponies and set off with the hound to Moss Hall where the Master, Colonel Swift, lived. The prospect made us nearly forget how hungry we were and how late it was.

'We didn't see much of the hunt,' said Ann. 'I wonder what happened?'

(A few days later we learned that they had lost three foxes, and that they wouldn't draw again because all the distinguished visitors wanted to get home before dark, and altogether it wasn't a very good run, so we hadn't missed much. At least the one thing we did miss which we might have enjoyed was the sight of Susan Pyke sitting in the middle of a mud splash where her too-large horse had deposited her, and picking bits of thorn hedge out of her hair. A few days later she told everybody at school that she thought hunting was silly and she only did it to please her father. Ann and I nobly forbore to tell her that the hedge she had brought down with her was one that our ponies had jumped easily; she wouldn't have believed us any way.)

Meanwhile we were riding home in the misty darkness, and it was quite dangerous as cars kept passing and sometimes the drivers yelled things at us, which was horribly rude and they might have discovered our unfortunate circumstances first.

Then it began to rain. We were soaked to the skin in addition to being filthy and starving. The only thing that kept us going was the thought of the book-like things that would be happening to us when we took the hound home tomorrow.

It was eight o'clock when we crawled into Chatton and our parents had roused the village to organize a search party for us. You can imagine how popular we were. My mother behaved quite well considering all things, but Mrs. Derry wept all over Ann, which was very shaming.

I said, 'When you hear all you'll know we weren't to blame,' in a very heroine-ish sort of way.

I then explained how we had saved the life of the Master's favourite hound and nearly worn ourselves out in the process.

'And tomorrow,' I said, 'we're going to take him to Moss Hall, but he'll have to stay at the cottage tonight.'

'But where is the hound?' said Mrs. Derry. 'I don't see any hound.'

Will you believe me, neither did we! There just wasn't any sign of the hound, beyond my lucky string, broken at the end where it had been round his neck. Just *when* he had got away I don't know. I had had him at the main crossroads and Ann had had him when we were nearly at Chatton, so whether he had escaped in the general hullabaloo of our arrival one couldn't tell.

Ann was quite ready to go off and find him, in fact so was I, because cold and hungry as we were we couldn't bear not to have the prospect of returning him and getting the enormous feed and the gold tie-pins at Moss Hall, but our heartless parents wouldn't hear of it.

So we were dragged off to our respective homes and fed and soaked in baths, and we spent rather a miserable night, alternately sleeping like the dead and wondering what had happened to Ranter.

What had happened to Ranter was eventually revealed. He wasn't the Master's favourite hound. He wasn't Lord and Lady Prance's favourite hound.

He wasn't in the hunt at all. He was recovering from hard-pad and was boarded out at the farm where Ann had borrowed the fork from the woman she thought wasn't pleasant, and when he escaped from us he made his way home and they never even knew anything had happened to him.

But worse was to follow. The woman at the farm complained to the Master that a girl from the Hunt (which Ann certainly was not) had called and borrowed a fork and hadn't even had the good manners to take it back but had left it out on the common where it had been picked up dirty and rusted. Every woman in the Hunt took this to heart (including Susan Pyke) and began to say, who could it have been, and poor Ann nearly pined away with her guilty secret. It was as bad as being sent out of the field for unsportsmanlike behaviour.

I wondered what I could do about it, and then to my surprise one Saturday morning I saw the Master himself, going into the corn merchant's in Chatton main street. Without thinking I shot in after him, and because I didn't know how on earth I was going to speak to him I just got in his way as much as possible in the hope that he would speak to me.

After he had fallen over me about five times in a very patient way I couldn't bear it any longer and squeaked, 'Oh, I am sorry!'

'You seem to be rather all over the shop, young woman,' he said, not unpleasantly, and I was so overcome that I stepped backwards into a sack of Spratt's Ovals and brought the whole lot down. As I staggered

about, I managed to capsize a pile of cat powders
and nearly finished up in a meal bin.

'I say, what *is* this?' said Colonel Swift.

I shoved my hair back with the front of my arm (my
hands were full of cat powders) and said all in one
breath, 'Oh, I must tell you, it was me – I – that
forgot the fork, not anybody from the Hunt.'

'I beg your pardon?' he said.

I went on like a river in spate, 'I sent Ann to the
farm for the fork and I'd never have forgotten it but it
was dark by the time we'd dug the hound out, and
there's been such an awful fuss and it wasn't anything
to do with the Hunt, it was me, and then the hound
got away so we hadn't anything to show, and I'm so
glad I saw you because I simply had to explain,
because of Ann.'

'I don't exactly follow you,' said the Master, 'but
I'm getting a glimmer. Is this something to do with
the day of the meet? You're not telling me you followed hounds, or did you?'

'In a sense, yes,' I said, 'but actually no, because
chil I mean, juniors weren't allowed, but we kept
catching up with the laggards and had to hold back
so as not to be really in the field.'

'Excuse me,' interrupted a woman rather coldly,
'but could I possibly get served with some duck rings
as I have to catch a bus?'

I thought for a minute the Master was going to
wave me aside and insist on being served, as it was
really his turn, but to my amazement and delight he
stepped aside and said, 'If this is anything to do with

the meet I want to hear about it. Now, young woman take a deep breath and try and tell me what you're talking about.'

So I poured it all out. It sounded a frightful jumble and my breath was coming in what the books call thick pants (I'd always wondered what that was, and now I knew), but I managed to tell him everything that had happened on that dismal day.

'So all the trouble arose from having given up a lot of time to tracing and digging out a hound trapped in a rabbit hole,' he said thoughtfully. 'No one ever told me that.'

'Nobody knew,' I said. 'The ghastly hound got away and went back home and we hadn't any evidence.'

'Let me see, what's your name?'

'Jill Crewe,' I gasped, and with terrific presence of mind added, 'and I represent Mrs. Darcy's equitation establishment.'

'And a very good place to represent too,' said the Master to my delight. 'I've noticed that the boys and girls turned out by the excellent Mrs. Darcy are neat and sportsmanlike, and they can ride.'

Will you believe me, this interview was so much like a fairytale already that I flung caution to the winds and the next minute I was telling this distinguished and magnificent man all about the Boost Mrs. Darcy club.

He smiled and said, 'Young woman, you needn't worry. I'll tell you something for your encouragement, worth always wins in the end. Don't envy other people, never show bad feeling or resentment, just stick at your job of riding in the very best way you possibly can. Good riding and good manners are never showy but they will stand the test of time, while showy riding and false manners fade out and disappear. You can tell your school-friends what I say.'

'Oh, I will!' I gasped. 'Gosh, I think you're wonderful!'

He smiled in the nicest, most understanding way, and I was so overcome that I stood on one leg and wiggled the other about, and over went the Spratt's Ovals again. Then he burst out laughing and so did I, and when the shopman not unnaturally looked a bit peeved, Colonel Swift just said, 'We seem to be knocking your dog biscuits about. Just send the whole sack up to my house, will you?'

Then, believe me or believe me not, this highly distinguished man and I left the shop together and I would have given anything for the whole school to have seen me at that moment.

He then shook hands with me – me! – and said finally, 'Tell your friend Miss Derry not to give the matter another thought. Neither she nor you have a stain on your characters as horsewomen and I'm extremely grateful to you for your public-spirited action in digging out the hound. Good luck with your riding!'

'Oh, thank you!' I gasped.

I stood there muttering 'thank you' long after he was gone, and then I pelted off to tell Ann and Mummy, and I wouldn't have changed places with the Queen of England.

7 - Just ducks

You may or may not remember that while I was in the corn merchant's a woman came in to buy rings for ducks. I hardly noticed her at the time but she turned out to be Diana Bush's aunt who had a farm at Corbridge a few miles away, and I little knew that I was one whom Fate had destined to put those rings on those ducks.

When I told my friends at school about the amazing interview I had had with the M.F.H. at first they could hardly believe me, but as the meaning of his noble words dawned upon them they realized that this was the best boost the Boost Mrs. Darcy Club had ever had.

The next Saturday Diana asked me to ride over to Corbridge with her to see her aunt's farm.

'It will be a good ride for Rapide,' she added.

Yes, I was riding Rapide at last. I had put in a good deal of work on him and he was responding quite well, and though I couldn't make myself feel very fond of him I had to admit that he hadn't let me down.

I would much rather have ridden Black Boy that

Saturday, but Diana had said Rapide – it was amazing how all my friends seemed to be such supporters of my peculiar pony – so Rapide it had to be.

Saturday was a glorious day, still and golden, and though the trees were bare their branches made a lovely lace-work against the blue sky. It was the sort of day you would like to get in the summer, but don't.

Rapide looked almost happy and when Diana presented him with an apple she had brought for him he flapped his eyelashes at her as much as to say, 'Come, things are looking up.' We rode gaily along the grass verge of the road towards Corbridge, and Diana told me that her aunt, Miss Bush, was a bit weird but very kind-hearted, which I think is a good way of describing most aunts. She ran this farm on lines of her own which were so odd that she couldn't get any experienced people with fixed ideas to work for her, but that didn't worry her. She was a whale for work and went at it herself from five in the morning to eleven or so at night, and was always full of beans and saying things like, 'Cheers, chaps!' and 'Up, boys, and at 'em.' She usually had some friend with farmy ideas staying with her, and they would work together as long as the friend could stick it. When she had had enough another friend would turn up, and so it went on.

'Mummy said I was to be sure and ask if there was anything I could do to help,' said Diana, 'so don't let me forget. If I forget, cough at me or wiggle your nose or something. I suppose you wouldn't mind helping a bit?'

'Oh, I'd like to,' I said. 'Only I haven't much patience with hens.'

'I've always wanted to lead a bull,' said Diana. 'Preferably at a Show, but anywhere would do for practice.'

'All right, you can,' I said, as Rapide, enjoying himself, broke into a canter and carried me ahead.

'That was nice, Rapide,' I said, patting him encouragingly, 'so don't look as if you thought you'd done wrong.'

At last we came in sight of Miss Bush's farmhouse. It was just like ones you see in pictures, made of mellow red brick with twisty chimneys, with a porch over the door where roses had climbed in summer. Diana said that her aunt had made it that way, and had even twisted the once-straight chimneys, but I don't know whether that was strictly true. There was a cobbled yard and just a few small farm buildings, because Diana said the whole place was only about twenty acres, which I suppose is quite enough if you want to do farming in an odd way on lines of your own.

Miss Bush saw us from afar and came rushing out to greet us, and at once I recognized her as the woman who had asked for duck rings at the corn merchant's.

When I am going to meet anybody new I always make up my mind beforehand what they are going to look like, and as I am always wrong I don't think I can have much of what they call intuition. I had pictured Diana's aunt as tall and thin with a long nose and the peering kind of spectacled eyes that you would find in anybody who sat up at nights with sick cows by the light of a dim lantern. Instead she was short and thick, the same thickness all the way down, and she had a round red face and a thick tweed coat and skirt that was so thick it hadn't any shape in it at all, and wellington boots and a red beret on the back of her head.

She waved to us as though welcoming an ocean liner and shouted out, 'Cheers, chaps! Come and eat! Jolly nice ponies, what!'

We liked the idea of eating and we were soon sitting round a table putting away sausages and chips and baked apples with brown sugar in the middle, along with Miss Bush – who said everything was either ripping or topping – and a friend who was staying with her called Mrs. Dulbottle.

Diana and I were trying to hide our giggles over this weird name when Miss Bush said, 'Now where's that daughter of yours? I don't intend the good old chap to work herself to death and miss her meals.'

She then strode heartily to the back door and gave a yell of 'Mercy! Mercy!'

Diana and I nearly jumped out of our skins, thinking Miss Bush had been attacked, but suddenly there appeared a very lanky girl of about sixteen with a bucket in her hand, and it turned out that she was helping Miss Bush on the farm while she convalesced after some disease or other, and she was Mrs. Dulbottle's daughter and her name was therefore the unfortunate one of Mercy Dulbottle.

Diana and I were so sorry for Mercy, who seemed a bit dim – and who could wonder with a name like that? – that we didn't wince at being introduced as 'two ripping girls, one of them's my niece'.

After dinner Miss Bush jumped up, nearly knocking off her red beret which she had worn all the time, and cried, 'Come, come, my hearties, there's work to be done!'

This meant washing-up, which we quickly did, and then we all went round the farm. This didn't take long as there wasn't much to see, ten dairy cows in a sort of cowish place where they were kept, two pigs asleep in a dark corner, and a lot of hens that got under our feet.

Miss Bush kept telling us how happy she was and how this farm was the dream of her life come true, and I thought it was jolly nice that somebody's dream had come true and hoped that mine would – I mean, about being an M.F.H., etc.

We admired everything terrifically, and Diana said, fancy having a farm and no place for horses, whereupon her aunt explained that there had been two stalls but she had turned them into a garage for her car, and this struck us as such a soulless thing to do that we were smitten dumb, which was a good thing considering what we might have said.

Then we drifted back to the house, and Miss Bush said, 'And why aren't you two chaps at school this afternoon?'

We pointed out that it was Saturday, and she just said 'Oh,' as if she didn't bother about such mere things as the days of the week.

Suddenly I remembered that Diana hadn't said

anything about what her mother told her about asking if she could do anything to help, so I coughed several times and wiggled my nose.

Diana said, 'What's the matter with you? – Oh, I see! Auntie, is there anything we could do to help while we're here?'

'Oh, I say, chaps, that's simply topping of you,' said Miss Bush in her own peculiar language. 'I wonder now – by Jove, I have it! The ducks!'

She then explained that she had two dozen young ducks on Corbridge Marshes which needed ringing, and she simply hadn't had time to get over there and do them, but seeing we had the horses didn't we think it would be rather fun?

I didn't really see Rapide capering about on marshes in search of ducks, but Diana was thrilled at the idea, and as Mercy said she would like to come too, on her bicycle, we all set off. Mercy had the rings in a box in her breeches' pocket and very pretty they were too, made of mauve plastic.

When we first got to the marshes we couldn't see any ducks at all, but presently one came shooting out of some reeds and we all dashed after it. We soon caught it up and it looked scared to death, as well it might. By the time Diana and I were off our ponies Mercy – who preferred to dash out on foot – had caught the duck and we all assisted at putting the ring on its foot. Actually it took all three of us to perform this simple task, one to hold the duck, one to hold its foot, and one to push the ring over its knuckle – or whatever ducks call their joints.

When the ring was on it looked very pretty, and the duck looked quite self-conscious and vain, so we let it go and it whizzed out of sight.

It took us two hours to round up and ring eleven ducks. Then unfortunately we started catching the same ducks over and over again.

'We were mugs,' said Diana, 'not to put the ones we had ringed into that hut over there until we'd got the lot. This is the third time I've caught that green one with a squint. Let's start from now, putting them in the hut.'

So we started catching all we could, ringed or unringed, and Diana and I on our ponies carried them squawking madly to the hut and fastened them in.

At last there were only four ducks left to catch, and as dusk was falling it seemed an impossible task.

'There just aren't any more ducks on this marsh,' I said. 'They must have flown off to Africa.'

'Look!' yelled Diana. 'There are three together, in the reeds!'

We swooped down on the unfortunate cluster of ducks like Red Indians on the war-path. Our ponies seemed to be enjoying this game tremendously, even Rapide.

'Gosh!' I cried. 'Will you look at this?'

I held up the duck I had caught. It was wearing a mauve plastic ring.

'Mine has one on too,' said Diana. 'That's funny. We shut them all in the hut.'

What do you think? Mercy, who I told you was a bit dim, hadn't shut the door of the hut properly, and when we went back to see there wasn't a single duck left in there at all.

It was now nearly dark and we knew it was no good spending the next two or three hours rounding up ducks which were already ringed in the hope of catching four that weren't.

'We'd better get back to the farm,' said Diana. 'Anyway, we've done our best. I wish we could have finished it and got those other four. You'll have to come down and have a go by yourself, Mercy.'

'Oh dear, it's all my fault!' said Mercy miserably, sounding as if she was going to cry.

'Oh, buck up,' I said, 'and don't be so dank.'

I know it was rather cheeky of me to talk like this to

somebody sixteen, but strangely enough Mercy did buck up – as I could not have done with a name like that – and told us a lot of funny stories which were very funny indeed, though I couldn't remember one of them afterwards. Isn't it funny how you never can remember funny stories when you try to tell them to anybody after?

Listening to the stories we weren't looking where we were going, which is silly on a marsh, and Rapide and Silvia were soon up to their knees in a bog. They stuck there, and while Mercy stood and yelled, Diana and I had to flop off into the bog and drag our ponies out. By this time most of the bog was on us and we carried it home. It was rather smelly bog too, and Mercy kept saying, 'Oh dear, you do hum!' which made us sorry we had been kind to her.

When we got back to the farm we told Miss Bush the whole story and how sorry we were about the other four ducks that we couldn't catch. Mercy didn't let on about leaving the hut door open, which we thought she might have owned up to, seeing we were so late.

'How many did you ring?' said Miss Bush.

'Twenty.'

'Well, that's all there were, my hearties,' said Miss Bush with a beam.

'But we've got four rings over,' I gasped. 'You said there were two dozen.'

'Two dozen rings, I meant,' she said, pulling off her beret, wringing it about in her fingers, and putting it back crooked on her head. 'Not two dozen ducks, old chap. Only twenty.'

'Can you beat it?' said Diana, as we trotted home through the dark lanes with red rear lights at our stirrup leathers. 'And now I expect we shall get into a row for being late home. That's what comes of helping people.'

However, when we got to our cottage fortunately Mummy was out and had left the key on the hook in Black Boy's stable and a note on the kitchen table to say she had gone to the Women's Institute. So we rang up Diana's mother and fortunately she had gone to the Women's Institute too, so nobody ever knew what time we got back. We made dripping toast for tea – at least I made it while Diana obligingly rubbed down both our ponies and gave them a feed – and we sat over the fire and ate, and it was gorgeous.

'I was just thinking,' said Diana, 'if I had to marry somebody called Mr. Dulbottle what I should call my daughter. I think something frightfully harmless like Mary, so you'd hardly notice it at all.'

'Or else something terrific like Veronica or Esmeralda that would bang people in the eye before they had time to catch on to the Dulbottle part of it,' I said. 'Anyway, not Mercy.'

'She was a blot, wasn't she? But it was a smashing ride and the ponies loved duck-hunting. Didn't Rapide do well?'

'He wasn't bad at all,' I admitted.

8 - Our Christmas

CHRISTMAS came, and Mummy had kept her promise to give me two loose-boxes. The old stable was pulled down, and while this was being done we could eat nothing at the cottage but boiled eggs as the wind was our way, laden with lime, mortar, ancient dust, and bits of everything under the sun. However, the new place was simply superb with its own little harness room and fodder room, and the doors were painted green, and it was the most magnificent present anybody ever had.

With Black Boy's head looking out over one half-door and Rapide's over the other I was so impressed that I tried to draw a picture, and the artist helped me and put in all the finishing touches.

Then I invited all my friends to come for tea and the official opening, which was performed by Martin Lowe who taught me to ride. Mr. and Mrs. Lowe came too – you have read about them in my other books – and Mrs. Darcy and Zoe and Wendy, and all my school-friends and some of their parents. After the opening which was out of doors of course, Mr. Derry, Ann's father, gave us a talk on horsemanship and always considering our ponies before ourselves, then Mrs. Darcy was asked to make a speech and she said, cheer up, it wouldn't be long until summer and the pony shows, and then we all went inside the cottage and had an enormous tea with iced Christmas cake and mince pies.

Mrs. Darcy started telling everybody the story of Rapide and the Disgusting Penberthys, realizing too late that this was all news to Mummy.

'Oh dear,' she said. 'Have I dropped a brick? I only wanted people to know that Jill has done a good job on this pony who had such a bad start in life.'

'Jill, you never told me this,' said Mummy. 'Is it really true that poor Rapide was badly treated? I remember how the day he came I offered him a carrot and he didn't seem to know what to do with it. How pathetic! To think that nobody had ever been kind to him before!'

'I think that people who can be unkind to ponies ought to be slowly tortured to death,' said Ann indignantly.

'No, that isn't the right way,' said her father. 'They must be taught to be more thoughtful and understanding. Cruelty to animals is more often thoughtlessness than deliberate beastliness, and it is up to you children to teach and educate other youngsters in kindness, and to give your whole-hearted support to all organizations that work for animals' welfare.'

'I haven't been as nice as I should to Rapide,' I confessed to Mummy after all our guests had gone, 'because I resented the fact that he didn't seem to like me, but that wasn't his fault and I ought to have been more patient. I don't think I shall ever love him as I do Black Boy, but I am getting fonder of him, and now he's got the idea that I'm not a blackhearted horse-butcher we may see some results. I used to think his action was very queer, but when Zoe rides him he doesn't look bad at all.'

'I thought he looked very well indeed, when you were riding him yesterday,' said Mummy, and knowing that she would not flatter or say anything that wasn't strictly true I was quite relieved.

After this superb Christmas present she had given me I felt that anything I gave Mummy would be an anti-climax. However, I had saved three pounds of my last summer's prize money on purpose to buy her something rather special, and I spent it on a very rich-looking white brocade cushion for her bedroom from a shop that appeared to be the kind of place that furnished palaces.

It was worth every penny of the three pounds when I saw this queenly cushion sitting on the blue chair in Mummy's room, and she was thrilled and kept walking round it and touching it and saying it was the crowning touch to her blue-and-white room, because though we live in a cottage our ideas are not entirely folk-weavish.

As for my other presents, by some strange trick of fate they nearly all turned out to be handkerchiefs. As I opened mysterious parcels in the cold light of that Christmas dawn and more and more handkerchiefs fell upon my bed I began to think I was under a spell, like people in fairy-tales. Of course I could understand getting handkerchiefs from rather soulless people like my Aunt Primrose and my cousin Cecilia (of whom you have read in my previous books) and handkerchiefs I got, six white linen ones of a rather dainty size with a white J. for Jill in the corner; but when it came to Ann Derry I just couldn't guess what she was thinking about! The six she sent me were jolly big ones and would come in for stable rubbers, but why shouldn't a horsy person *send* another horsy person stable rubbers and have done with it?

Mrs. Lowe, Martin's mother, had also sent me handkerchiefs. Seven of different colours with the name of the day of the week in the corner, upon which day I suppose that particular handkerchief had to be used. I began to wonder if some awful Fate would befall the careless person who used the wrong handkerchief on the wrong day. In any case it would probably put you off pretty badly if you pulled out your handkerchief and found it said Monday when you knew perfectly well it was Saturday.

When I went into Mummy's room and told her about all these handkerchiefs she laughed like anything and said it was a judgment on me for all the hundreds I had lost in a long and energetic lifetime. Then we heard Mrs. Crosby (No Relation to Bing) letting herself in downstairs and I went down to give her her present. Then she gave me what she had brought for me, which was a handkerchief, an enormous yellow cotton one with red horses' heads all over it. Apart from the fact that I have never seen a horse with a bright scarlet head and an expression like a dying parrot, the whole thing was very practical, and because it was so large I could see it coming in useful for all kinds of emergencies, even for joining a broken girth if I should ever be so unlucky as to suffer such a frightful disaster.

I might add that not all my presents were hand-kerchiefs. For instance, when I opened Diana Bush's parcel I found she had given me a tin of saddle soap, which is a jolly good present for any pony-owner, only it happened that my present to Diana was also a tin of saddle soap.

I found that with two ponies to look after I now had to work very hard, but it was worth it. I exercised them in turn, because I found they both hated being led while I rode the other one, and on Boxing Day morning it happened to be Rapide's turn.

It was a good morning for riding and Rapide was very cheerful, which in this case took the form of throwing his head and making faces. I soon discouraged that and we cantered along happily on the grass verge. Just as I was thoroughly enjoying myself I saw somebody leaning in a miserable sort of way against a field gate and chewing the stalk of a dead chestnut leaf.

It was Wendy Mead, the girl who helped Mrs. Darcy with the riding school.

'Hullo, Jill,' she said in the dim sort of way one does say hullo when one is not enjoying one's self and other people are.

I drew in Rapide, who looked around as much as to say, What on earth are we stopping for?

'What's the matter, Wendy?' I said.

'Oh, nothing,' she said. 'Only Mrs. Darcy has had a telegram. She has to go and look after her brother's horses in London while her brother has an operation, so it means the riding school will be closed for about a fortnight. You see, there's only me and Joey and all we can do is look after the ponies. It'll be awfully dull.'

'What about Zoe?' I said.

'Oh, didn't you know? Zoe went home for Christmas and she isn't coming back. Her people want her.'

'I call that rugged,' I said, and rode on thoughtfully.

About half an hour later I met Diana Bush and her brother James coming back from a ride over Neshbury Common and I told them the news.

'Oh, but the riding school can't possibly be closed,' said Diana. 'People will hate to miss their lessons, especially those who are keen on entering for the Hunter Trials. And some of the beginners might even leave and go to Lime Farm if they can't get their usual lessons. I think it would be disastrous to close the riding school for a whole fortnight. We've nearly got a new pupil for Mrs. Darcy too, haven't we, James? A boy who's come to live next door to us.'

'I think it would be disastrous too,' I said. 'You remember those notices we put in the new girls' desks and got kept in for? Well, they weren't all wasted because Rhoda Richardson –'

'Rhoda *who*?'

'That tall girl with big ears in Four A. She's much nicer than she looks. She said that if her mother would let her learn to ride after Christmas she'd go to Mrs. Darcy's. Well, it's after Christmas, isn't it?'

'It's the Christmas holidays,' said James, 'when naturally everybody wants to have a lot of lessons.

It's pretty awful if a riding school isn't open in the holidays.'

James spoke very knowledgeably as he was sixteen and had won Class C jumping at Chatton Show the previous summer, which I think was a terrific achievement.

'Listen,' I said in an inspired sort of way. 'What's to stop us running the school ourselves if Mrs. Darcy will let us?'

'Us?' said Diana looking a bit stunned.

'We could, you know,' said James. 'The more experienced riders mainly want to practise the sort of jumps they'll get in the Hunter Trials and I know all about that sort of thing, so I could at least help them a bit, and you girls could manage the beginners blindfolded. It would be something to do and we'd get heaps of riding.'

'Oh, do you think Mrs. Darcy would let us?' said Diana. 'I mean, we are pretty experienced and we know her ways of teaching –'

'Let's go round there and see,' I said, beginning to feel very excited.

When we confronted Mrs. Darcy with the idea she started making difficulties, as people over the age of forty always seem to do as a matter of course, though perhaps I am libelling Mrs. Darcy in suggesting she was over forty. I don't think she could have been really, as she was quite healthy and not at all bowed with age. However, underneath it all I could see she hated the idea of having to close the riding school for a fortnight and was ready to grasp at any straw.

'I don't suppose you could do any actual harm,' she said slowly. 'But you'll find it rather a bind.'

'Oh, no, we shan't,' we all said in a chorus, and Wendy Mead started brightening up and said she thought it was a whizzo idea.

'Well, provided your parents consent you can try it,' said Mrs. Darcy, and we all said there wasn't a doubt about their consenting as they liked to see us doing something useful in the holidays.

So it was all arranged and we spent that evening writing postcards to all the pupils saying that lessons would continue as usual in Mrs. Darcy's unavoidable absence, under the tuition of well-qualified teachers, with particular attention to those who wished to practise for the Hunter Trials.

On the first morning after Mrs. Darcy had gone we all turned up at the stables before it was light, so as to give Wendy a hand and to look keen. I came to the conclusion that there is nothing gives you the needle so much as responsibility, but as the day wore on Diana and I got into the way of things and didn't do anything awful, and James was so busy building his jumps that we hardly saw him.

You would hardly believe that there were human beings so dim as to be practically incapable of keeping their heels down, or their knees up, or their hands down or their heads up, and yet I seemed to be coping with such people hour after hour. The beginners weren't so bad, they were at least humble, but it was the people who had had three lessons and thought they could ride who gave all the trouble. There was one girl called

Jennifer Jackson who actually tried to canter with her toes down, her elbows out like teapot handles, and her chin sitting on the knot of her tie, and just as I was going to tell her how truly awful she looked she piped out, 'Mother says that now I can ride she's coming to watch me.'

I feared that if her mother should see what I saw she would collapse and die.

I said, 'Jennifer, do hold your head up. I've told you before.'

Jennifer gave a lurch which caused her unfortunate pony to stagger – he was her own pony – and said, 'There! That's what happens when I try to hold my head in that awkward position you taught me.'

'Of course that will happen,' I said, trying to sound calm and cool, 'if you don't keep your heels down.'

'If I keep my heels down,' said Jennifer rather crossly, 'my knees sort of come up.'

'So they should,' I pointed out. 'And do put your elbows to your sides, Jennifer.'

'Oh, I can't ride like that,' said Jennifer. 'I feel like a brown paper parcel.' And off she went again, looking *exactly* like a brown paper parcel that is coming untied.

I felt very hot indeed by tea-time, much hotter than Diana who had had quite a good time with the Shetland pony crowd, aged six or seven.

'You've had the best of it,' I said.

'Don't you believe it!' she said going bright red. 'I had one little beast who yelled, "Hold the nasty pony's head like Nanny does while I get on!" It turned out that his big fat Nanny practically smothered the pony with both arms and her apron while the horrible child climbed up him as if he was a stone wall. I was simply livid. I said, "Nobody's going to hold the pony's head, and it's you that's nasty, and either you learn to mount him decently or you needn't bother to come here any more." '

'Oh, I say, you'd better be careful,' I said in a fright. 'Supposing he doesn't come any more! We simply can't afford to lose any of Mrs. Darcy's pupils, even if they are little beasts.'

'Yes, Di, you've got to be frightfully tactful when you're running a riding school,' said James coming up. 'I've found that out already. You should have heard me! I think I'm destined to be an ambassador or a royal courtier or something. I had people this afternoon who've got as much chance of completing the course at the Hunter Trials as I have of winning the open jumping at Earl's Court. But I just took a big swallow and said, "Quite good, quite good".'

'Then I think you're a galumphing great hypocrite!' said Diana to her brother. 'You're downright dishonest and that's one thing you can't be in a riding school, isn't it, Jill?'

'Well, I think you can sort of strike the happy medium,' I said and Diana said, 'What's a medium anyway, and why should it be happy, and how do you strike it when you can't see it?'

9 - Running the riding school

THE next day we made a duty rota, so that we shouldn't all be working at the same time, and Wendy and I went on for the afternoon.

'Help!' said Wendy. 'Here come the Fisher twins – *and* their mother!'

I didn't know the Fisher twins, who turned out to be a boy called George and a girl called Georgina who were ten years old and brought their own ponies, which were beautifully groomed, not by them it turned out but by their father's groom. All their tack was new and beautiful and shining, the sort of tack I'd have all the time if I could afford it.

Mrs. Fisher was small and fair and all smiles, but she had rather a warlike expression.

'I thought I'd come along with the children,' she said, 'as Mrs. Darcy isn't here. I want to see that they're properly taught. It's so important that they shouldn't learn anything the wrong way at this stage.'

'I'm going to begin jumping today,' said Georgina, who looked much more like a boy than George, who looked much more like a girl than Georgina.

'Oh, but you can't,' said Wendy. 'You've only had four riding lessons.'

'But I don't agree with that attitude at all, not at all,' said Georgina's mother, looking sweet in a rather

horrid way. 'I think it's so wrong to check a child and Georgina doesn't know fear. Why, the first time I was ever on a horse I was only seven years old. My uncle picked me up and put me on his great black mare, and said, "Away you go" – pointing to a hedge that must have been over five feet high. And of course, knowing no fear, I just clung on and over I went, like a bird. After that I could jump anything.'

T—D

During this improbable story I stood with my mouth slightly open, but when Mrs. Fisher had finished Wendy had the presence of mind to say in a matter of fact way, 'Well, Georgina won't go over anything like a bird so long as she keeps on losing her stirrups. Look at your feet, Georgina! And do try to keep your heels down. Anyway, you're not nearly ready to jump.'

'Yes, Georgina, you really must keep your heels down, dear, and I think it's quite wrong of Miss Wendy to tell you to look at your feet. Mrs. Darcy always says, keep your head up,' said Mrs. Fisher.

'I didn't mean it like that,' said Wendy going scarlet.

'Now that's very nice, Georgina, very nice indeed!' said Mrs. Fisher. 'Come along, dear. Sit well back.'

'You mean, sit well forward,' I said, quite unable to bear this.

Mrs. Fisher glared at me, and said, 'Now dear, let Mother see a smart trot.'

I thought, who's supposed to be giving this lesson, anyway?

But Wendy firmly took Georgina's rein and said, 'Let's start from the beginning again. Georgina, your seat is awful and your hands are anywhere but where they ought to be. You look as if you were playing the piano.'

She then began to get Georgina organized and just when she had got her into something like a decent position the horrible child said, 'If I can't jump I'm not going to ride. I'm going home.'

'Oh no, darling, oh, you must be a good girl!'

cried Mrs. Fisher, dancing round in a flappish sort of way. 'Do it nicely, just for Mother.'

'I won't,' said Georgina, and began to slither off her pony, while Mrs. Fisher grabbed her and tried to push her back. Wendy and I stood by helpless, looking at this awful exhibition and thinking what we would do to Georgina if we could have her alone and at our mercy for five minutes.

After a good deal of undignified heaving Mrs. Fisher won the day, and when she had Georgina back in the saddle looking like a sack of potatoes with a scowl on its face, she turned to us panting and said, 'She's so highly strung, that's the trouble. You have to know how to deal with her. But highly strung people make the very best riders. I'm sure she's going to be wonderful. I do hope you'll keep on telling her that, Miss Wendy. Highly strung people need such a lot of encouragement.'

'If you want me to go on with the lesson,' said Wendy, keeping her temper remarkably well, 'we'd better go back to the beginning, and first of all I shall want Georgina to walk a circle.'

'I don't want to,' said Georgina with an even heavier scowl. 'It's babyish. I won't walk a circle.'

'Need she?' said Mrs. Fisher. 'I mean, it's like being a beginner all over again, isn't it?'

'It may surprise you,' I said, chipping in, 'to know that even the best riders usually begin schooling by walking a circle. It's good for the pony.'

'Georgina darling,' said Mrs. Fisher, 'do walk a circle, just to please Mother.'

'I will if I can jump afterwards,' said Georgina stubbornly.

I'm afraid I should have told her to take her Frightful Little Self straight home, but Wendy who had a great deal more patience said, 'All right then, I'll put a bar at eighteen inches and you can try, if your mother wants you to. You'd better come with me now, and walk a circle.'

'Oh, all *right*,' said Georgina rather rudely, and starting off jerkily followed Wendy to the marked out circle in the level field that was the riding school.

I realized now with a sinking heart that I was left to cope with George, who all this time had been sitting on his pony fiddling with some Meccano parts.

'I must tell you about George,' said Mrs. Fisher. 'I think he's rather special. I'm not saying that because he's my own child, but I do think he has the look of a first-rate rider, and I feel that with the right coaching he'll be able to compete with *anybody* when the gymkhanas begin next summer.'

'How many lessons has he had?' I asked.

'Six.'

'He's got quite a long way to go,' I said tactfully.

'Ah, but wait till you see him,' said Mrs. Fisher proudly. 'He's going to win every single event next summer, aren't you, George?'

(I hope not! I thought.)

George put the Meccano parts in his pocket and sat up very straight on his pony. He certainly looked much better than his sister.

'Look at his hands,' said Mrs. Fisher. 'Beautiful.

So light and sensitive. You have to be born with hands like that.'

George's hands didn't look any different from any other beginner's hammy ones, but I didn't say anything.

'He's much more advanced than his sister,' said Mrs. Fisher. 'Come along, George, let's see some action.'

Action was hardly the word for what happened next. To my horror, for I had been in a kind of daze up to now, I saw that George carried a full-size hunting crop and this he brought down with a whack on his unfortunate pony's flank, and off they went at a pace I can only describe as an uncontrolled lope with George bouncing about in the saddle and using his beautiful, sensitive hands every now and then to push himself off the pony's neck.

'Isn't he spirited?' said Mrs. Fisher.

'He's got a lot to learn,' I said firmly. 'For one thing, he isn't allowed to use a hunting crop, or even a stick while he's schooling. And for another you can see the daylight between his legs most of the time. And he mustn't stick his feet out like that! And he hasn't really got a bit of control over his pony – look at that!'

George's headlong career had brought him to the verge of colliding with his sister's pony, now walking in a passable manner round the circle under the direction of Wendy. He leaned back and dragged on the reins, the pony threw back his head in an outraged sort of way and dipped his haunches, and the next minute George was rolling about on the grass.

'If he did that at a gymkhana,' I could not resist saying, 'everybody would die with laughing.'

That really did make Mrs. Fisher look a bit worried.

'I'm afraid he'll have to go a bit slower,' she said, 'but he'll find it very boring.'

At this point Wendy came to the rescue and said, 'Look, Mrs. Fisher, I really think it unsettles the children to have you watching. Couldn't you come back for them later?'

I held my breath for fear Mrs. Fisher would refuse, but after a moment she said, 'All right. I'll come back in half an hour. But do give them a really good lesson. I mean, if it's just riding round and round in a circle they can do that at home.'

I refrained from saying that if they would do that at home they'd probably begin to learn a little bit about the principles of riding, and off she went.

After that we got on a bit better. George wasn't a difficult boy at all when I got him alone, and though he had so many faults that I hardly knew where to begin he was keen to learn. Meanwhile Wendy put the bar down to eighteen inches and gave Georgina a little elementary instruction about how to sit when jumping. Georgina needless to say took no notice at all, leaned well back, put down her toes, and when by a miracle she found herself on the other side of the jump and still on her pony's back she yelled, 'I've done it. I told you I could. Now put it up to a proper jump.'

'Let's do it,' I said to Wendy, 'just to take her down a peg.'

'Daren't,' said Wendy. 'She'll break her neck.'

'That wouldn't be a great loss to equitation,' I muttered.

However, with her usual great patience Wendy raised the bar to two feet, and George bounced over it gaily, nearly standing in his stirrups, and flopped back on his unfortunate pony's withers with a re-sounding slap.

Then Georgina tried, lost her stirrups, slithered over her pony's tail and lay on the ground till Wendy went and picked her up.

'Are you hurt?' said Wendy coldly.

'No,' said Georgina.

'Then you should get up by yourself. And now perhaps you'll realize that you can't jump before you learn to ride.'

'I jumped,' said George. 'I was jolly good.'

'If you jumped like that in a competition,' I said, 'your pony would give you three refusals next time and you couldn't blame him. You looked frightful.'

'Did I?' said George with a faint gleam of intelligence.

'Look,' I said, 'I'll show you how to do it.'

I took Georgina's pony – not George's which showed signs of terror – and did the jump in a reasonably competent way.

'I'll do it like that,' said Georgina. 'Show me how.'

'Not now,' said Wendy firmly. 'Ponies aren't machines and can't go on for ever, especially after the knocking about you give them. If you two are sensible and want to be real riders you'll do just as we tell you in future. Get it out of your heads that you can ride already because you can't. You're terrible, both of you, whatever your mother says. Now do you want to ride properly so that you can enter for competitions and not disgrace yourselves, or don't you?'

'Yes,' muttered George. Georgina said nothing but looked a bit more interested.

'Right,' said Wendy. 'Come tomorrow at the same time, and come by yourselves if possible, and we'll have a proper lesson. Now let me see you mount your ponies and sit exactly as I tell you to.'

They both mounted, not too well, but Wendy got them into position, heads and knees up and heels and hands down.

'There!' she said. 'You look quite decent. To-morrow you will walk, looking like that. Then in time you will learn to trot and canter, still looking like that. Eventually you will also learn to jump, still looking like that. You get the idea?'

'Yes,' said George.

'Georgina?'

'Yes,' said Georgina.

'You can tell your mother,' said Wendy, 'that you've had a good lesson this morning. I can see her coming. You can go and join her. Slowly!'

George and Georgina rode away at a snail's pace. They didn't look bad at all.

'Oh Wendy you are marvellous!' I said. 'I do think you're a good teacher.'

'Whew!' said Wendy, fanning herself with both hands, 'A bit more of that would have killed me.'

By now I had begun to admire Wendy.

'What do we do next?' I said.

'Let me see,' she said, 'I'd better exercise Blue Smoke for half an hour.' (Blue Smoke was Mrs. Darcy's own gorgeous hunter.) 'There's a boy called Tom Vale waiting for a lesson, over there. Could you take him? He won't give you any trouble. He does everything you tell him and he's very slow.'

'Do you mean dim?' I said, my heart sinking into my boots.

'No, it's just that he doesn't want to ride and his people make him. He's ready to jump really, but he'll probably pretend he isn't.'

I felt rather sorry for Tom Vale as I saw him coming towards me, looking rather like a cockerel going to its doom, if you know what I mean. He had on breeches and boots that were too big for him. His black velvet cap was also too big for him and his brown tweed coat was much too long. His tie was pulled so tight it creased his collar, and he was very round-shouldered.

I said, 'Hallo, Tom, have you got your own pony?'

He said, no, he usually rode Mrs. Darcy's Picture.

I said, 'Well, I thought you'd have got him out and saddled by now.'

He said, 'O.K., I'll go and do it,' and shuffled off. I got the idea he was trying to put off the evil day.

After about ten minutes he came riding out on Picture.

I said, 'Does it take you ten minutes to saddle up?'

He said, 'Yes, usually.'

I thought, Help!

He sat quite well, but didn't attempt to do anything.

I said, 'What do you want to do today, Tom?' and he said he didn't know.

For this lack of keenness I could have bitten him, but I just said, 'Well, do a collected walk round the circle,' and he did it, correctly, but looking as if he was about to go to sleep.

I said, 'Now show me a trot.'

He started off on the wrong leg, and I brought him back and made him do it properly. He just did it, in a quite mechanical way. He then went right round the circle at a very nice collected trot and came back and stopped by my side. By now poor Picture looked as bored as her rider.

'Miss Wendy says you're ready for jumping,' I said.

'No, I'm not,' he said.

'Look here, Tom,' I said, 'you ride quite well. What's the matter with you?'

'Nothing,' he said.

'It can't be true,' I said, 'that you don't want to ride?'

'Well, I don't,' he said.

I just gasped.

'It's Father,' said Tom. 'He wants me to go in for jumping competitions so that he can watch me, and I'll never be able to. I'll just make a fool of myself.'

Then it all came out. Will you believe me, poor Tom had never seen boys of his own age jumping? His father had taken him to Earl's Court to see first-rate show-jumping and had calmly said, 'There! That's what you've got to do.'

Tom was naturally a scared sort of boy and had been very crushed at home, and he had panicked. He was only eleven and he had got the idea that he was going to have to compete with men.

I said, 'Wait a minute,' and I went and consulted Wendy.

I said, 'I know what's the matter with Tom. Tell me, quick, is there a boy of eleven who can jump? Somebody we could get hold of quickly?'

'There's Tony Adams,' she said. 'He's only ten –'

'All the better,' I interrupted. 'Could you phone him and ask him to come round here at once?'

'O.K.,' she said. 'What's the idea?'

To make a long story short, in about ten minutes Tony Adams came round. I recognized him. I had seen him jumping in children's classes the previous summer and he was quite good.

'Hallo, Tony,' I said, 'would you mind getting up on Picture and going round the junior jumps?'

'Could we have them down to two-foot-six?' he said. 'Picture's only 12 hands.'

So Tony and I dashed round and lowered the wall and pulled the top off the hedge and put the bar to two-foot six. Then Tom got down off Picture and Tony got up and away he went.

I could have found a few faults with his jumping, and he knocked a block out of the wall, but the point was he looked as if he was thoroughly enjoying himself and so did Picture. He did the three jumps three times each, and the third round he cleared them all beautifully and came back laughing, and patting Picture.

Tom was looking at Tony with his eyes popping and his mouth open.

'Thanks very much, Tony,' I said. 'How long have you been jumping?'

'Well, last summer was my first season in competitions,' he said. 'I got two seconds and a reserve.'

'What about it, Tom?' I said, with a grin. 'Would you like to try?' Tom gave a gulp and said, 'I'd like to do that, but it looks a bit high.'

'Of course,' I said. 'You'll start on the bar at eighteen inches. Come on, Tony, let's put it down for Tom.'

I could see Tom pulling himself together with a do-or-die look on his face, but he had the pluck to do just as I told him. There he sat looking rather pale, but his seat was right and so were his knees, feet and hands, and Picture took the jump like a floating feather.

When Tom realized that he had actually jumped, you should have seen him! He couldn't believe it.

'I like it!' he said, as though he had expected it to hurt him.

Tony and I started to shriek with laughing, and presently Tom joined in.

'Please can I do it again?' he said.

So he did it again, quite enthusiastically, in fact I had to tell him not to bounce.

'Can I come and have another lesson tomorrow?' he said. 'When are you coming again, Tony?'

I arranged to give them both a jumping lesson during the week, then I sent Tom to unsaddle Picture and give her a rub down.

'My Russian Rabbits!' said Wendy when she saw him doing this, looking so keen and excited. I told her what had happened.

'Well that's a feather in your cap, Jill,' she said. 'That boy has been coming here for weeks and we couldn't do a thing to rouse his interest. Why on earth couldn't his father have taken him to see some children's jumping instead of plunging him straight into Earl's Court and scaring him stiff? I shouldn't be surprised if Tom's a credit to the riding school in next year's events. I'd put his chances before George Fisher's anyway!'

10 - The three fats

THE next day it was the turn of Diana and James to take the teaching, but I couldn't resist going round in the afternoon to see how they had got on.

They had had a wonderful time. In the morning they had done a little competition with the Babies – which was what we called the under-tens, who were very docile and thought we were grown-ups – and in the afternoon they had collected all the people who wanted to do hacking and didn't want to do schooling, and taken them for a country ride.

'I must say, you've had a jolly easy day compared with mine yesterday,' I said.

'Oh no, we haven't,' said Diana, because people loathe to be told they've had an easy day.

'I had to do a lot of very tricky teaching,' said James. 'All that lot were simply frightful in traffic, especially a girl called Meadows.'

Wendy gave a shriek of rage, as she was very keen on Phyl Meadows.

'She *was* frightful,' said Diana, sticking up for her brother. 'Her pony was nervous about the bit where the road is up in Charlton Lane, and she hadn't a clue how to steady him down and get him round it. James had to take the rein and lead him.'

'You must have put her off,' said Wendy loftily,

'because I would say that Phyl Meadows is actually the best all-round rider we've got.'

'Coo!' said Diana.

'Doesn't say much for the others,' said James.

'My gosh!' said Wendy. 'What makes you think that you can come up here and criticize the riding?'

'Oh, chuck it, everybody,' I said. 'Either we're trying to run this place or we're not. O.K., James and Diana have had a very hard day. And tomorrow it's you and me, James.'

The first lesson for next morning was booked for 10 o'clock. I overslept and was late for breakfast. Then I spilt porridge on my jodhpurs, and couldn't find the Thawpit and knocked a lot of other bottles over, and Mrs. Crosby said if I was her girl things 'ud be different, that they would, and I said, 'What you said just now doesn't make sense'; and she said she was sick and tired of me mixing up the brown polish shoe-brush with the black polish shoe-brush and she sometimes wondered why she went on.

Just at that moment the telephone rang, and it was Wendy. She sounded rather excited and said, would I mind bringing Black Boy and Rapide with me, as there were three new pupils waiting for a lesson and no ponies for them.

'Help!' I said. 'They're not groomed. I got up late.'

'Well, bring them as they are,' said Wendy, 'and we'll have a go at them here. I'm terrified these three will go away again if they think there aren't going to be ponies for them.'

Fortunately, Black Boy and Rapide didn't look

bad. I gave them a quick brush over, and off we went. When I got to Mrs. Darcy's there was a scene of wild activity. The two ten o'clock pupils had arrived, and were mounted on the school's own ponies, Cocktail and Picture, while James walked them round the circle, and there before me, as though awaiting their doom and mine, were the three fattest girls you ever saw in your life. They were aged about twelve, eleven and nine and they looked just like bouncing balls. They were nicely dressed in very new looking jodhpurs and coats which looked strained to the uttermost. They said their names were April, May and June Cholly-Sawcutt, and their mother said they were to pay by the hour. Then they handed Wendy the money for their lessons.

I said, 'I don't think I've ever seen you before. Have you lived here long?' And they said, no, only about a fortnight.

Wendy said, how did they hear about the riding school, and April said that their father had asked their neighbour, Mr. Vale, if there was any establishment where they wouldn't mind teaching three great lumps to ride because he hadn't the strength himself, and Mr. Vale had told them to come to us and ask for Miss Jill, because if she could teach his son Tom to jump she could teach anything from a hippopotamus downwards.

My eyes nearly popped out, and Wendy said to the fat girls, 'Does your father ride, then?' And May said, 'Sort of.'

Wendy screwed her forehead up and said, 'I feel as

if I'd heard your name before,' and June said, 'Once heard never forgotten,' and then they all giggled and ended up roaring with laughter.

Wendy said to me, 'I'd better give you a hand with these three,' and she told Joey to saddle Patsy, who was a very sturdy pony, almost a weight-carrier.

Then we started to teach the three to mount. After half an hour the sweat was pouring off us and we were nearly deafened by their yells of laughter, but we had got them up. Black Boy and Rapide kept turning their heads to give me reproachful looks for doing this awful thing to them, though they only had to carry the two younger Cholly-Sawcutts, May and June. Patsy, who looked to be sagging, had April. We spent the next half-hour teaching them to sit properly and then we led them round the circle, while James who had finished teaching stood watching and nearly strangling himself to keep from laughing.

Actually the three girls were quite keen to learn and did everything we told them, only they looked so funny and they were so noisy. I could just picture them in years to come, riding to hounds and yelling till the echoes rang and the whole field was practically unconscious from the din, and being told to shut up by some mythical future M.F.H., possibly me.

When the hour was up Wendy and I were tottering, and Wendy said she would go and make the elevenses and we would have a heartening drink of cocoa before my next lesson.

When she got back the three fat girls had gone.

'They liked it,' I said. 'They thanked me. They're

coming twice a week, Tuesdays and Fridays, and they want to know if they can soon ride well enough to go on a Saturday afternoon hack. They'll be here on Friday at ten, and it's you and Diana to take them.'

Wendy was flapping her eyelashes with excitement. In her hand she held a copy of *Horse and Hound*, a back number, rather battered.

'Look,' she said. 'I can't believe it. I knew I'd heard the name before.'

There was a picture of a man in hunting kit. Underneath it said, 'Captain Cholly-Sawcutt of the British jumping team which has just returned from its triumphant Italian tour. His famous mare, Petronelle, has the distinction of never failing to win a place in any competition this season.'

'Do you think he's their father?' I said with a gasp.

'He'll have to be some relation with a name like that,' said James.

We could hardly wait for Friday, and at ten o'clock when the fat girls turned up for their second lesson we were all there, Wendy, Diana, James and I.

'Oh yes, that's Daddy,' said April calmly.

'But I asked May if your father rode,' shrieked Wendy, 'and she said, sort of.'

'Well, he only sort of rides,' said May. 'He jumps mostly.'

'You might have told us,' I said, 'that your father was practically one of the most famous men in the world.'

'We never thought you'd be interested,' said June. 'Can I ride Rapide today?'

We all helped the fat girls to mount, almost reverently.

'Clear off, you two,' said Diana to James and me. 'Wendy and I are doing this.'

James and I went and sat on a hurdle, dithering with excitement. Across the mild January air came shrieks of laughter as April, May and June Cholly-Sawcutt yelled encouragement to each other.

'Do you think their father will want to come and see how they're getting on?' said James.

'Shouldn't wonder,' I said. 'We'll get his autograph. The girls at school will go mad.'

'Don't you see, idiot,' said James, 'that the riding school's made for life? "Under the patronage of Captain Cholly-Sawcutt of the British Show-Jumping Team" – Mrs. Darcy can put it on her advertisements.'

'But are we?' I said, 'I mean, under his patronage?'

'Of course, you dope. He sends his daughters to be taught here. That's being under his patronage, isn't it?'

'I expect it is,' I said. 'But I don't think Mrs. Darcy will put it on advertisements. She hates showing off. She says that good riding is its own advertisement.'

'Well, she can't help being pleased we've got her the Three Fats,' said James. 'I hope she comes back soon before they fall on their noses in the thorn-hedge and we lose our reputation as teachers.'

'You'd better stop calling our star pupils the Three Fats,' I said. 'I wonder if there's the slightest chance of their father coming here? I'd die with excitement.'

We talked about the Cholly-Sawcutt girls for days, but though they came regularly for their lessons nothing else was said about their famous father and we didn't like to ask.

Meanwhile I was putting in quite a lot of work on Tom Vale. Tom and Tony had struck up a great friendship and wanted to have their lessons together, and of course nothing could have been better for Tom's riding. Nothing would hold him back. He had made up his mind to be as good as Tony in as short a time as possible, and the fact that Tony was a year younger than he was made him grit his teeth with determination. So Tom got on, and did easy jumps very nicely, and even clamoured for higher ones which I daren't let him try yet.

Then Rhoda Richardson turned up, the girl with big ears in whose desk we had put one of our doomed advertisements. She brought her own pony, at least it was her uncle's pony and he had lent it to Rhoda to learn to ride on. It was a strange-looking pony of a peculiar shade of yellow. It had a very large head, very thin legs, and a depressed expression which wasn't surprising since it had the unfortunate name of Treacle.

Rhoda's legs were too long for Treacle and she did look a bit comic, but as James said, she was a new pupil and we had got to treat her with respect.

He gave her her first lesson himself, and she tried very hard and turned out to be an awfully nice girl.

She asked when she would be able to ride well enough to go for a Sunday afternoon hack with the rest of us, and when she had left Diana said, 'Don't let her, James. She looks so frightful, she'll let us down.'

But James said coldly, 'I shall let her. She'd knock spots off you for keenness, and she's the most decent girl I've taught so far.'

He continued to stick up for Rhoda and Treacle,

and I must say they both made a lot of progress and Diana had to shut up, completely squashed. Which proves that you shouldn't laugh at people and think them comic.

Mrs. Darcy had hated to leave her hunter, Blue Smoke, and had weighted down Joey and Wendy with instructions about what she had to have and what she hadn't to have, and about what had to be done for her each day and at what time. Joey and Wendy carried out these instructions to the letter. They were always fussing over Blue Smoke, her oats and her blankets, her hay and straw; they spent hours grooming her and examining her feet, and if she had been a frail little baby they couldn't have measured out her food more carefully.

Every day when it was fine Blue Smoke had to have just the right amount of exercise, no more and no less, and only Wendy was allowed to mount her.

Blue Smoke's exercise nearly drove James, Diana and me frantic. To see that beautiful mare ambling round the paddock, for ambling is the only word to describe the pace allowed by Wendy, while passers-by leaned over the gate to watch, was nearly more than we could stand.

One morning while Wendy was dealing with a rather sticky pupil and Joey was leading out the hunter shiningly groomed and blanketed, James said, 'Let me exercise Blue Smoke, Wendy, while you go on with the lesson.'

'Oh no, James,' said Wendy. 'Nobody's supposed to ride her but me.'

'But that's screwy,' said James. 'Honestly speaking, Wendy, who is the better rider, you or I?'

'Well, you are, of course' – began Wendy, realizing what a lot of prizes and cups James had won in his long riding career and how he had finished with children's classes and would be in open classes next season.

'You admit that,' said James, 'and Mrs. Darcy knows it, and you know that Mrs. Darcy knows it. So it stands to reason that if you can ride Blue Smoke I can.'

'So what?' said Wendy.

'Oh, go on, Wendy, don't be so dim! Let me take her round, just once.'

I think Wendy wanted to avoid being thought stuffy by James, whom she rather admired, so she said, 'Well, only for five minutes, and do be careful.'

James ran off eagerly, and the next minute he was up on Blue Smoke. He looked marvellous and he knew it. He walked the gorgeous mare round the circle, then put her to a canter and did a perfect figure of eight. Wendy couldn't help admiring James's performance, while keeping one eye on the lesson she was giving.

James rode up and dismounted, patting Blue Smoke's neck.

'Oh, James!' I said. 'Could I get up? Just for one minute. I've never sat a hunter like Blue Smoke and I've always dreamed of it.'

'Why not?' he said. 'She's too tall for you, but I'll give you a leg up and adjust the leathers.'

When I found myself actually mounted on Blue Smoke it was the thrill of my life. I walked her very carefully, dithering with excitement and nervousness. By now Wendy had got her pupil down at the far jump and wasn't noticing James and me.

'Wouldn't you like to try a jump?' said James. 'The bar's at three foot and she can do five easily.'

'Gosh, no!' I said. 'I'm coming down.'

I slid down, not too cleverly, and said, 'Do you think she's had enough?'

'Enough!' said James. 'This mare isn't getting enough exercise to keep her ordinarily fit.'

Just at that moment Wendy called me to settle an argument between herself and her pupil. I went haring up the field where the jumps were.

'Ruth says that these jumps aren't as difficult as the ones we shall get in the Hunter Trials,' said Wendy.

'Of course they are!' I said. 'Mrs. Darcy told me that if anything they were a bit stiffer.'

'I rode in some Hunter Trials last year,' said Ruth – who was a girl who was always telling you about the marvellous things she had done at other places – 'where the jumps would have made these look like baby's first lesson. But that was in Leicestershire where they really ride.'

'I wouldn't bother with our Hunter Trials, if I were you,' I said sarkily. 'I mean, nobody over the age of three goes in for them, actually.'

'If you think these jumps are too easy, Ruth,' said Wendy, 'I suggest you let me see you do a clear round and then I can judge what you are capable of.'

Ruth piped down at once, because she knew perfectly well she couldn't do a clear round of our practice jumps.

Suddenly Wendy gave a shriek. I nearly jumped out of my skin and turned round to see if there had been an explosion or something.

All I saw was James on Blue Smoke, sailing over the five foot hedge which very few of us have ever attempted. He looked magnificent. It was a perfect jump with inches to spare, and he made a perfect landing.

'James! Get down this minute!' yelled Wendy. 'Get down, you idiot. Oh!'

'All right,' said James, calmly, dismounting with a smile. 'Keep your hair on.' He patted Blue Smoke, and said, 'You'd like more of that, wouldn't you, old girl?'

Wendy rushed up and took Blue Smoke by the bridle.

'You'd no business to do that, James,' she said furiously.

'It hasn't done her a bit of harm. Don't be so stuffy, Wendy.'

Wendy said no more, but led Blue Smoke away and handed her over to Joey.

The rest of the morning things were a bit strained, as Wendy was huffy and James was sulking, but I didn't care. All I could think of was how it felt to ride a wonderful hunter of sixteen hands, worth five hundred guineas in actual money and about a million pounds in pride to her owner, and I started making mad plans to save five hundred guineas. At the rate of five guineas a year – which would be about all I could manage – it would take me just a hundred years. (I wasn't very hot at arithmetic, but even I could do that sum.) I would be a hundred and fourteen years old when I got my hunter. It didn't seem worth the effort.

11 - Trouble at Ring Hill

MUMMY was very interested in what we were doing at the riding school. She used to say she could hardly wait for each evening to hear about our adventures and our pupils, ghastly and otherwise.

On this particular evening I didn't say anything about Blue Smoke as I felt a bit guilty, and I was afraid Mummy would rub it in as even the best of parents seem as though they can't help doing. I rubbed the ponies down, fed them and put them up for the night. Then I sat over the fire and read a book called *Tschiffely's Ride* which you ought to read if you haven't read it already, as it is about a man who rode two horses across Central America.

Then I had some cocoa and buns and went to bed. Mummy sat up to alter a chapter in her new children's book, which was even more whimsy than usual and still called *Angeline, the Fairy Child*. I mean, much as I admire Mummy's skill as a writer, can you *imagine* anybody called *Angeline, the Fairy Child*? But the publisher was clamouring for Angeline, and the American rights were already sold, so it just shows that it is true what Shakespeare or somebody said, that half the world doesn't know how the other half lives.

I had been asleep and woke to hear the telephone ringing. It felt like the middle of the night, but just then the grandfather clock downstairs struck eleven and I heard Mummy answering the phone.

I heard her say, 'But Jill's in bed and asleep by now, Wendy.'

Some frightful premonition chilled the blood in my veins, as it says in books. I tore downstairs in my pyjamas.

'Is it Wendy?' I said. 'Please let me speak to her.'

'I don't know what she's thinking about, ringing up at this time of night,' said Mummy, in a very parentish voice. 'And you must not rush about the house without your dressing-gown, Jill.'

But I had already grabbed the phone and said in a gasping sort of voice.

'What's the matter, Wendy? This is Jill.'

'Oh Jill!' said Wendy, as if she was crying. 'It's Blue Smoke. She's ill. What shall I do? *Do* come up here!'

I went cold all over.

'Mummy,' I said, 'Wendy wants me to go up there. Blue Smoke, Mrs. Darcy's hunter, is ill.'

'But you can't go up there in the middle of the night! Tell Wendy to send for the vet.'

'You don't understand,' I said. 'It's my fault about Blue Smoke, at least partly. I must go. I simply must.'

Mummy stood there looking slightly stunned while I tore about looking for some clothes and a mack and shoes.

'Jill, you *can't*,' she kept saying.

'I've got to,' I said, bashing my way through the kitchen cupboards in search of my bicycle lamps and feeling certain that the batteries would be finished. I found the lamps and they weren't very good, but they did light.

'I think it's perfectly ridiculous,' said Mummy, being thoroughly grown-uppish and not at all understanding, which wasn't really surprising considering I hadn't told her anything she could understand. 'Racing about the lanes in the middle of the night!'

'I'll be as quick as I possibly can,' I promised. 'I'll just help Wendy to get the vet.'

I rode off into the dark with my bike wobbling all over the place. It was the most frightful moment of my life. I had visions of Blue Smoke being dead when I got there. I couldn't think of anything that I or James had done that could upset her, but we must have done something. I felt ghastly.

I found Wendy sitting on the ground in Blue Smoke's stall, between two lighted hurricane lamps, with Blue Smoke's head on her knee. Wendy had been crying. The mare had her eyes shut, every now and then she quivered and gave a slight moan.

With pedalling furiously up the hill I had stopped being cold all over, but now I went cold all over again.

'Is she dying?' I gasped. 'Where is she hurt?'

'I don't know,' said Wendy, stuttering with cold and misery. 'I've felt her all over but I can't find anything wrong. Oh, why did I let James ride her! Now she'll die and I shall lose my job here and never get another.'

I quite saw Wendy's point, it was awful.

'I can't think of anything that James did to her to cause this,' I said. 'He rides so well. And,' I added miserably, 'I was on her myself for about two minutes. I can't think of anything I did.'

'It must be James's fault,' said Wendy. 'She was all right before.'

'Have you sent for the vet?' I said.

'Yes, of course I rang him, and he's out at some farm with some sordid cow. His wife said she'd send him here if he came back in time.'

'In time for what?' I said.

'In time for Blue Smoke still being alive, I suppose.' Wendy began to cry very splashily.

I sat down in the straw and sadly stroked Blue Smoke's cheek. She opened her eye and gave me a dismal look of woe. I felt frightful. I was sure she was very ill indeed and though I didn't see how it could have been James's fault and mine I was sure it must be. Mrs. Darcy would never have anything more to do with me, the future looked so black.

Joey came creeping in with some colic medicine, just in case it was colic that was the matter with Blue Smoke, but when she had had it she didn't seem any better. Anyway, she didn't seem to have colic. I thought of that hideous bit in 'How we brought the good news from Aix to Ghent,' where it says, 'All of a sudden the roan, rolled neck and crop over, lay dead as a stone.' I couldn't help wondering if jumping the five-foot hedge had done to Blue Smoke whatever it was that riding from Aix to Ghent had done to the roan.

We were all very miserable. I went into the house and phoned Mummy to tell her that I was staying the night with Wendy. I didn't tell her we were spending the night sitting on the ground in Blue Smoke's stall.

'I think you might have sent for James as well as for me,' I grumbled.

'I did,' said Wendy. 'But his father answered the phone and said James had gone to bed and he wasn't going to give him any message at that time of the night. I know James would have come if he'd known. He'll be furious tomorrow when he knows.'

I couldn't even bear to think of tomorrow.

I suppose we must have fallen half asleep, because suddenly a big torch was shining in our faces. The vet had arrived.

'Now what's the matter with Blue Smoke?' he said. 'Can't be much. She's usually fit as a fiddle.'

'I think she's dying,' said Wendy. 'We both think so.'

'Well, you girls clear out,' said the vet, cheerfully, 'and let me have a look. Go and make me a cup of tea. I've been sitting up with a cow for hours.'

We thought it was very heartless of the vet to want tea, but we went into the house and made him a cup. We didn't make any for ourselves, it would have choked us. Every time I caught Wendy's eye she gave a gulp, and every time Wendy caught my eye I gave a gulp. We did nothing but gulp at each other. Outside we could hear Joey shuffling up and down in the yard.

I set off down the yard with the vet's cup of tea and it slopped all over into the saucer.

'You dope, you're spilling it all,' said Wendy.

'Well, carry it yourself if you're so clever,' I said.

Then suddenly I saw the vet before me. The heartless man was grinning all over his face.

'She's just been playing you up,' he said. 'A touch of toothache, that's all, but you know these thoroughbreds are all nerves and at the least touch of pain they act as if they are dying.'

'Are you sure?' gasped Wendy. As for me, slosh! – down went the cup of tea all over the flags.

'Of course I'm sure. I'll show you where her gum's swollen. I've put a touch of something on it and she's O.K. already.'

We followed him into the stall. Blue Smoke was up on her feet and looking very sheepish. She nuzzled Wendy's arm and made a whiffling noise.

'Gosh!' said Wendy. 'She's asking for apples. You fraud, Blue Smoke!'

The vet lifted her lip and showed us the swollen gum.

'When's Mrs. Darcy coming back?' he asked.

'Not till the end of the week.'

'Oh, that's all right,' he said. 'She won't take any harm for a week and then we can get the tooth examined. It may only be a bit of cold.'

'Could it possibly be with riding her?' I asked anxiously. 'She was jumped this morning.'

'Do her good,' said the vet cheerfully. 'She's not getting enough exercise by a long shot.'

So that was that. It was now one o'clock in the morning, an hour at which I had never been up before.

It felt very peculiar. Joey fastened everything up and I went back with Wendy to her house. I don't know if I mentioned before that she lived at the farm next to the riding school.

We let ourselves in by the back door of the farm, which was never locked. The farmhouse was about six hundred years old.

Wendy said it felt like a good opportunity for seeing the ancestral ghost who – or which – was a headless yeoman riding a headless mare down the stairs, but he – or it – didn't appear and I wasn't sorry as I felt much too tired to cope with ancestral ghosts.

We both got into Wendy's four-poster bed and fell fast asleep. Mrs. Mead woke us at seven next morning and it didn't feel a bit nice getting up. I went straight home to find Mummy far from pleased about everything, and I did see her point and agreed with all she said. I didn't want to be stopped from going to the riding school.

I changed, and went up there about eleven. James was there, and wasn't a scrap impressed with the story of our sufferings which Wendy had poured out to him. He rather pooh-poohed the whole thing and said we were pretty dopey not to know when a horse was dying from some internal injury and when it merely had toothache. We rather hated James.

However, we couldn't keep it up for long, as he was full of an idea he had for a field ride which would be good practice for the Hunter Trials. He had fixed it for the Wednesday afternoon and had got permission from the farmers whose fields we wanted to cross – which you should always do if you are planning a field ride.

As only the experienced pupils were taking part in the ride we knew it would be fun and not much trouble.

I had been keeping my two ponies at the school because of the work they were doing with the new pupils, and the night before the ride Wendy said to my surprise, 'I say, Jill, could I ask a favour?'

'Of course,' I said. 'What is it?'

'Would you let me ride Rapide tomorrow?'

If she had asked me to let her ride an elephant I couldn't have been more surprised.

While I was still gasping in a fishlike way she went on, 'I've been schooling him quite a lot when you weren't here. I've had him over the practice jumps heaps of times and I like him. I'd love to ride him tomorrow, and I know you're going to ride Black Boy.'

'Gosh!' I said. 'You can ride him with pleasure but I don't know why you want to.'

'You'll know why tomorrow,' she said.

It was a mild sunny day next day for the ride and not at all like January. Eleven of us turned out and we had grand fun. The ponies had the freedom of the fields which they loved, and we jumped low hedges and any sort of natural hazard such as you get in Hunter Trials.

When I saw Wendy going over everything on Rapide you could have knocked me for six. I had put in a bit of schooling on Rapide myself, but this was magic. The pony had quite lost his miserable, suspicious looks and was enjoying himself as much as the others. And his peculiar action in jumping wasn't nearly so marked as it had been. He certainly could jump.

Afterwards, when we were rubbing down, Wendy said, 'Had you thought of jumping Rapide in the Hunter Trials?'

I said I hadn't.

'I think you're crazy not to enter him,' said Wendy. 'He's got tremendous pluck and he's a born jumper. You really haven't given him a chance.'

'I don't know if he'd do for me what he's done for you,' I said, rather humbly.

'He would if you'd give him the chance. If I were you I'd put two months' hard practice in on Rapide and stop being so distrustful about him.'

I didn't say anything but I was quite impressed by what Wendy said, when I remembered what she had been able to do with Rapide. I had to admit that I hadn't done my best with him, and I had always ridden him for duty and Black Boy for pleasure. So I expressed my regrets to him that afternoon with a bit of petting and an extra handful of oats.

I was cleaning out the bucket in the harness room when I heard someone behind me. I jumped up and saw two men who looked vaguely like people's fathers.

'Am I addressing Miss Jill Crewe?' said one of them, who was tall and thin and a bit like Danny Kaye when he isn't smiling.

'That's me,' I said.

'Stand back a bit,' he said. 'You're something of a curiosity.'

I thought perhaps he was a bit screwy, so I stood back and wished I didn't look so dusty and unhorsemanlike, with most of my hair in my right eye.

'Behold!' he went on. 'The girl who taught my son to like riding!'

'Oh,' I said. 'Are you Tom Vale's father?'

'I certainly am,' he added. 'I've been singing your praises as a teacher far and wide.'

'I'm not really very good,' I said. 'Tom rode well before I had him but he just didn't take any interest until he saw other boys of his own age doing things. I think it was jolly unkind,' I added, carried away by my feeling, 'to show him what show-jumpers did at Earl's Court and expect him to do the same. It would have put me off for life.'

When I had said this I realized how rude it sounded and wished I hadn't, but Mr. Vale only smiled in a feeble sort of way and the other man said, 'Bravo, I couldn't agree more.'

'Anyway,' said Mr. Vale, 'I've recommended your riding school to a lot of people and you'll be overwhelmed with pupils soon, I fancy.'

'But it isn't my riding school!' I yelled. 'You should see Wendy Mead, she's an absolutely magic teacher, and it's really Mrs. Darcy's riding school only she's away, and she's the best teacher in the county, only people go to Lime Farm to Captain Drafter's because he teaches their horrid children to bounce about on ponies and their ghastly parents think it's smart –'

I gasped for breath, wondering what awful things I

was going to say next, but the man who wasn't Mr. Vale smiled nicely and said, 'Well, you won't have to suffer from Captain Drafter's establishment much longer. He got into trouble, owing money all round the district, and he's packing up and getting out. Honesty is the best policy, as they say.'

'Gosh, yes it is, isn't it?' I agreed warmly.

Just then harsh peals of laughter rang out behind me and the ground seemed to rock. Only one person on earth could have a laugh like that. It was April Cholly-Sawcutt.

'Miss Jill doesn't know it's Daddy!' she chortled. 'She doesn't know it's Daddy!'

My legs nearly gave way under me. Was I really talking to the great hero of the show ring, Captain Cholly-Sawcutt himself? I was!

My head spun round and round and I said 'Oh!' Then I shouted, 'Please, please, please wait till I fetch Wendy! She must see you! We do want your autograph. And James too. And Diana.'

At the same time I was afraid to go away in case he should vanish, but just then Wendy came along and we both shook hands with the great man, feeling dizzy with excitement. It was quite the greatest moment of my career.

Wendy said, 'I'd give anything to see Petronelle.'

'Why not?' said Captain Cholly-Sawcutt very obligingly. 'Supposing I bring her round on Saturday afternoon? Some of your pupils might like to see her too.'

We couldn't believe our ears. The moment the

distinguished visitor had gone we rushed off to find
Diana and James who were having tea at home.

At first they thought that we were having them on,
because things like having Captain Cholly-Sawcutt on
Petronelle coming to your riding school on a Saturday
afternoon don't happen except in the sort of dreams
you get after eating too many mince pies on Christmas
Day, but when they found it was true they couldn't
eat any more tea and Diana went quite white, and Mr.
and Mrs. Bush took a dim view of the proceedings; so
we cleared off and I went home at ninety miles an hour
and told Mummy the whole thrilling story.

12 - A great day for all

You'd be surprised to know how quickly the great news went round. Half our school stopped Diana and me in the street and said, 'Is it true that Captain Cholly-Sawcutt is going to be at Mrs. Darcy's place on Saturday, with Petronelle? Could we come and see him?'

Yes, we said, it was true, but of course there would only be room for people belonging to the riding school. Practically everybody then rushed off to ask their mothers if they couldn't join the riding school before Saturday, and we had to make a rule about fees in advance.

Finally who should come along but Susan Pyke who had always looked down on us and had been the star pupil at Lime Farm Riding School.

'Hallo, Jill,' she said in a frightfully friendly way. 'I hear you're having Captain Cholly-Sawcutt on Saturday. I've met him before, you know. I suppose it's all right if I come along?'

'I'm afraid it isn't,' I said. 'We only have room for Mrs. Darcy's own pupils. But if you wait at the field gate,' I couldn't resist adding, 'you might see him go by.'

Susan crumpled up a bit, but said it really didn't matter as she'd be seeing a lot of Captain Cholly-Sawcutt in the future when she rode at Earl's Court, possibly next year, and I said, 'How lucky for you,' and Ann Derry who happened to be with me said, 'You ought to pal up with April, May and June. They'd be just right for you.'

'Are they up to my standard?' said Susan, and Ann said, 'The question is, are you up to theirs?'

On Friday we collected all the pupils and gave them instructions about being properly dressed and having their ponies perfectly groomed. We started the grooming Saturday at seven o'clock in the morning, washed tails, polished hoofs, scrubbed and cleaned and had everything looking magnificent by lunch time. We couldn't eat for excitement.

By two o'clock all our pupils were assembled and we held an inspection. They looked very nice indeed after we had re-tied everybody's ties and made them re-rub their boots and put their hats on straighter. Even George and Georgina Fisher looked quite decent, and when Tom Vale stood up straight he didn't look a bit round-shouldered and his clothes seemed to fit better. Wendy and I brushed each other's coats till we were quite exhausted.

'Gosh, look at all the people in the lane!' said Diana.

I think half Chatton was lingering outside the paddock, as if waiting for royalty, and there were dozens of autograph books held in people's expectant hands. Even Susan Pyke had swallowed her pride and was sitting on the top rail of the gate with an open book in one hand and a fountain pen in the other.

'I've booked in twenty-seven new pupils,' said Wendy, who was quite tomato-coloured with excitement, 'and they're all taking a minimum of twelve lessons, starting from next week.'

'He's coming!' shrieked James.

And up the drive through the paddock rode Captain Cholly-Sawcutt himself, on Petronelle, that famous show-jumper.

I can't describe what a wonderful time we had. Picture it for yourself! He signed all our books and let us pat Petronelle, and then he told us about his experiences in the show-jumping world and gave us a short lecture on equitation which we all drank in eagerly, and then he finished up by jumping Petronelle round our jumps. It was like a fairy-tale. All the people in the lane had a good view too.

We were so taken up with watching that none of us noticed a taxi ploughing its way through the crowd. Something made me turn my head, and there coming up the paddock was Mrs. Darcy, tottering slightly and looking quite overcome.

I raced to meet her. She looked at me in a dazed sort of way.

'Is it a fire?' she said. 'Or is somebody being arrested?'

'Look!' I gasped, pointing to the magic figures of a horse and rider flying over our five-foot rail fence.

She passed a hand over her face.

'I'm going mad,' she said. 'Do you know, Jill, I actually thought I saw Captain Cholly-Sawcutt on Petronelle jumping the five-foot in our field.'

'Yes, you did,' I said. 'It's him.' (Which is bad grammar.)

She ran both hands through her hair.

'I'm quite crazy,' she said. 'I must be. I thought I came home, and there was an enormous crowd at the gate, and Jill Crewe told me that Captain Cholly-Sawcutt on Petronelle was doing the jumps in our field. I must be in the last stages.'

'You're not mad,' I said. 'It's happening. I can explain everything. Look, here's Wendy. We'll tell you all about it.'

'After this,' said Mrs. Darcy, 'nothing that you could do, Jill – nothing! – could cause me the slightest surprise.'

Then she went and shook hands with the hero, whom she had met before in the show ring, and everybody talked at once, and we had a gorgeous time. After it was all over, and Captain Cholly-Sawcutt had praised the riding school and thanked us for the way we were teaching April, May and June to ride, which was a thing he couldn't have faced attempting himself, and had promised to come again some day, he went off and we calmed down a bit.

'And now,' said Mrs. Darcy, 'somebody might tell me just what's been going on.'

We didn't know where to begin. For about a minute we stood with our mouths open and not a sound came, then all of a sudden we all began talking at once and then we couldn't stop. We told her about the Three Fats and how they turned out to be the daughters of the famous rider, and about Tom Vale, and about all the new pupils. We told her about Blue Smoke's toothache, and believe me, she laughed.

When we had finished and were gasping for breath she looked rather awkward, and then said, 'I just don't know how to thank you.' Which was a tremendous lot, coming from Mrs. Darcy.

We all fidgeted and said things like, 'That's quite O.K., we loved it,' and then she said briskly, in her old way, 'Well, thank goodness you'll all be back at school next week.'

The thought was a bit blighting.

'We know,' said Diana. 'But after all it's only eleven weeks to the Hunter Trials.'

I don't remember much about what happened at school that term, except that we had a Careers Week. This was an invention of Miss Grange-Dudley, our headmistress, and was for everybody in the school of thirteen or over.

In the afternoons instead of the usual lessons we were to have talks on careers by people who had done them, and as well as the talks everybody had to have an interview with their mother and Miss Grange-Dudley in the head's room, which sounded to us simply awful.

'I'll bet you all the talks are about humdrum things like domestic science and nursing,' said Ann as we biked home together. 'There couldn't possibly be anything decent like air hostesses or breeding cocker spaniels.'

The fact was, Ann had definitely decided either to be an air hostess or run a kennel. Actually, nearly every girl in our form wanted to do something with dogs or horses except for a rather dim girl who wanted to run a teashop, and one who wanted to be a gym mistress, and one who wanted to be an explorer after reading a library book called *Two Girls and a Tandem in Tibet*.

Ann was quite right. The talks were all very dull except for one on Ballet by a woman who had been at school with Miss Grange-Dudley and had something to do with Sadler's Wells, and as she kept on saying you couldn't begin too young and preferably at about eight, it didn't seem to be much use.

There wasn't a single Career talk that even mentioned dogs or horses, you'd think they didn't exist.

Ann went for her interview before me. She came out looking a bit hopeless.

'What was it like?' I said.

'Awful,' said Ann with a groan.

'Did you tell her you were going to be an air hostess? You said you would.'

'I couldn't get it in,' said Ann. 'First Miss Grange-Dudley made a speech, the same one she makes every speech day, and when she stopped for breath Mummy chipped in about wanting me to know about antiques so that I could run an antique shop, and when she'd done they both looked at me and said, Well, that's all settled, and the next minute I was outside and it was over.'

'You feeble thing!' I said. 'You ought to have interrupted.'

However when it came to my turn I found it wasn't so easy to interrupt. But just when I was getting desperate Mummy said in her nice way, 'When all is said and done, Jill is the one to decide. I should like her career to be entirely her own choice, and whatever it is I shall help her in every way.'

I gave her a huge smile and knew that everything was going to be all right.

'And what does Jill want to do?' said Miss Grange-Dudley in a sort of here-come-the-horses voice.

I had made up a speech about the three things I wanted to do all at the same time, being an M.F.H., and an M.P. so that I could get some decent laws passed for horses and other animals, and all the rest, but when I came to the point all I could get out was, 'I want to run an orphanage.'

Miss Grange-Dudley was so surprised that she nearly fell off her chair.

'Well!' she said. 'That's very praiseworthy of you, Jill. It's the unexpected that always happens.'

'A jolly sort of orphanage,' I said.

'I've always thought,' said Miss Grange-Dudley, 'that you had it in you to become a writer like your mother.'

This was a new idea for me and I thought it was terrific. Yes, I *would* be a writer, but not like Mummy. I would write pony books! I could hardly wait to get home to start. It was wonderful to think I had found a career I could begin at once while I was waiting to be old enough to do my other three things.

On the way home I bought a writing block, and directly after tea I began my first book which I called *Jill's Gymkhana*. You have probably read it.

13 - The hunter trials

I WOULD like to be able to say that the day of the Hunter Trials dawned bright and fair, because that is what it would have been like in a proper book, but truth compels me to relate that it was raining. When I first opened my eyes I could hear the steady drip-drip, but I pretended I was dreaming it and jumped up and rushed to the window. Everything looked wet and misty.

However rain or no rain it was Hunter Trials day at last and six o'clock, so I got into my old jodhs and mack and tore down to start on my ponies. It is a bit discouraging to groom and polish horses and wash their tails and comb and plait their manes on a wet day because you think perhaps it is all going to be wasted after all and they will eventually arrive at the scene of action looking like draggled rats. I tried not to think of it like that, but thought instead of all the other people I knew at this moment who were also grooming and washing and polishing and combing and plaiting.

Isn't it funny how well you can plait on days when it doesn't matter, and when it does matter the plaits come out looking like something you tried for the first time in your life?

I dashed about, oiling hoofs, washing tails, flourishing a stable rubber. When Black Boy finally looked like patent leather and Rapide like polished mahogany I tied them carefully so that they couldn't spoil themselves and went into the kitchen to see about breakfast.

'There's nothing like hard work in a good cause,' said Mrs. Crosby.

'It's a good cause all right,' I said. 'Hunter Trials. We've all been waiting for this for ages.'

'Never heard of it,' she said cheerfully. 'What do you do?'

'Oh, just jump over things,' I said.

'Well, don't you go bringing no more silver cups home for me to clean,' she said.

'Not much hope,' I said. 'It's mostly for grown-up people and big horses. Only two children's events and I don't stand an earthly in either of those. Mrs. Crosby darling, could I have an awful lot of porridge this morning?'

'I'm doing you two eggs,' she said kindly.

'Angel!' I said. 'While you're doing it I'll clean my boots, and then there's the ponies' lunch to pack and mine.'

'Ponies' lunch!' she said.

'Oats,' I said. 'And please, Mrs. Crosby, could you look for my fawn tie and I can't find the hat brush either.'

She said I'd lose my head if it was loose, and I couldn't think of a reply to this as I had my mouth full of porridge and was looking for something to make myself some sandwiches for my own lunch at the same time.

Mummy came in and said, 'Now don't get too excited. Isn't it time you went up to dress?'

'Oh, Mummy,' I said, 'you might look for my fawn tie. It isn't in the drawer.'

'There's something else that isn't in its proper place,' said Mrs. Crosby, coming in with my bowler all covered with dust. 'In the glory hole under the stairs, it was. I'd better give it a brush. You'd lose your head if –'

'Yes, do brush it for me,' I said, 'that is, if you can find the hat brush, I can't.'

'It's a good thing you look after your ponies better than you do after yourself, Jill,' said Mummy, discovering my fawn tie in the knife drawer.

In the end I found the hat brush in the harness room. All the time I was dressing I was wishing it would stop raining, and when by the time I was ready I found it actually had stopped I couldn't believe that one of my wishes had come true. It still looked very damp everywhere but it wasn't raining.

'Rain before seven, fine before eleven,' said Mrs. Crosby who was very good at little mottoes and things like that.

'You look very nice,' said Mummy. 'I do hope you don't have to ride in a mack.'

'I shan't in any case,' I said. 'Are you sure my jodhs are the same fawn as my tie?'

'Identical,' she said. 'Really, you horsy people are so fussy.'

She was coming later in the Lowes' car to watch, and bringing the lunches and the grooming tools.

By the time I got to the course the weather was brightening a little. Several of my friends were already there, and Diana was moaning because her pony, Sylvia, hated wet ground and never did much good except on dry.

'The course,' said James, 'is awful. Downhill and uphill.'

'Well, that's what you'd get in hunting,' said Ann, 'and Hunter Trials are supposed to reproduce natural hazards you'd find on a cross-country ride.'

'Thanks for the information,' said James rather huffily.

Everybody we knew seemed to be there, and they all looked much better mounted and more confident than we did, but this is something that one always feels at the beginning of competitions.

Ann and I rode round to look at the course and loosen up our ponies, as the first class was the children's class in which, with a lot of misgivings, I was riding Rapide. Of course I had put in a lot of practice on him, but it was the first competition for which I had entered him. Spurred on by Mrs. Darcy, Wendy and everybody else, I couldn't do otherwise, but I didn't think much of my chances and was looking forward more to riding Black Boy with Ann in the partnership.

There were eight jumps for the children's class and two more were to be added for the open classes. Five of the jumps were gorse fences. Two were plain, one downhill and one uphill; two with water on the take-off side, and one that gave me the needle, with a ditch on the landing side. Ann said it didn't worry her, the one she hated was the uphill one. There was also a brook to be jumped twice, going out and coming in, and a natural in-and-out formed by a grassy lane with low hedges.

By the time the steward called us into the collecting ring and began to explain the course to us I for one was past caring. I was quite sure I was going to have three refusals at the first fence, or else no refusals but about 28 faults.

I could see Mummy and the Lowes at the rails as the first competitor, a girl called Madge Madden, took off. We all held our breaths and watched, as one always does watch the first competitor.

Madge didn't have a very good time. She did an enormous jump at the first fence where it wasn't necessary and a feeble one at the first water jump where she got 4 faults. We lost sight of her at the in-and-out which was in a sort of a dip, and when she did reappear she got three refusals at the uphill fence and that was the end of her. I felt very sympathetic.

Diana was next.

'She's taking it too fast,' said James who was standing beside us. 'Sylvia doesn't like wet ground but she needn't rush her along like that. There! She's crashed that easy fence with her forelegs!'

Diana collected both herself and Sylvia after that and seemed to do quite decently, but when she came back to us she said she had got at least 12 faults.

'Didn't you clear the brook both ways?' asked James. 'I couldn't see you properly but I thought you did.'

'I did going out,' said Diana, 'but coming back Sylvia went in with her hind-legs, and you know how she loathes wet. She messed up the uphill fence after that though it wasn't really hard.'

Jack Winsley, one of Mrs. Darcy's pupils went next. He was a very serious boy and rode so carefully it made you want to scream. He had no faults in six jumps, but he took ages over them and as he approached the seventh jump with the ditch on the landing side he realized he was losing time, which counted in this competition. He used his stick, his pony started to pull, crashed the jump and ran out.

Then a few more people we knew rode. Joan Bishop fell off at the brook, rolled into the water, led her pony out and retired. John Finch beat his pony round and then got three refusals which he deserved. Lulu Brown who was the youngest competitor and only ten did a beautiful round and only came to grief at the last fence from sheer excitement at doing so well. April Cholly-Sawcutt, who had insisted on riding her new pony though she was far from ready, got fifteen faults and then retired.

We heard somebody say, 'Lead me away and lay me down!' and it was Captain Cholly-Sawcutt with his hand over his eyes.

Ann giggled but she soon stopped, as it was her turn.

'Jolly good!' said Diana generously as Ann cleared the first two fences.

'Her timing's always so good,' I said. 'Oh help!'

Ann's pony had taken off too soon at the first water

jump and brought down bunches of gorse with his hind-legs.

However Ann had a lot of applause as she came to the finishing post and only had four faults.

'You're much the best so far,' I said, as she gave her pony oats.

'That's nothing,' said Ann. 'Look at Harry Forrester now.'

Harry Forrester was only two days off sixteen, and so was lucky to get into this event which was for *under* sixteens. He was a very experienced rider and had been in competitions since he was nine. His pony was a thoroughbred. All these things made us feel a bit nervous.

'But I've seen him do frightfully badly,' said James.

However Harry did frightfully well. He sailed over everything and got the first clear round. Everybody clapped like mad.

'You were terrific, Harry,' said James.

'It was only a fluke,' said Harry, who wasn't at all conceited but a very nice boy.

There were two more good rounds, people seemed to get better as the event went on, and then it was my turn.

As I felt Rapide gather himself for the first jump I knew he was going to do it. He sailed over with inches to spare.

I touched him between the ears, which meant in our language, you needn't overdo it. He took me too literally, and I felt his fore-feet catch the gorse of the next fence which was one with water on the take-off side. The next was all right and so was the in-and-out and we came up to the brook for the second time. Rapide jumped too high and I was sure we were going to miss the edge, but somehow we were down and cantering on to the uphill hedge.

This time I saw the gorse fly. I didn't think I had a chance now, so I didn't worry about the final jumps and strangely enough cleared them.

When I got back to the others Ann said, 'I say! You were marvellous.'

'I got either four or six faults,' I said.

'You didn't,' said Diana. 'You only got two.'

'But at the second jump –'

'You didn't bring anything down,' said James, 'so I think you've been lucky.'

Then we heard the loud-speaker say, 'Number 27, two faults.'

'Hooray!' said Ann. 'You're second to Harry Forrester so far.'

Of the remaining competitors there were two decent rounds. One looked to be clear, only there was some argument and we didn't hear the final result. It was done by a girl called Helen Moffat, one of Mrs. Darcy's pupils, and the other good round was by Jean Smith from Lime Farm Riding School.

You know how it is in a competition, you get muddled up with the results and don't know where you stand. When the judges began to call in and I heard 27 called I was quite surprised.

'Go on!' said Ann. 'I told you you'd done well, Jill.'

Harry Forrester was first, I was second, Helen Moffat was third, and Ann was reserve.

'I was certain Jean Smith had got it,' said Ann delightedly as we munched bars of chocolate and gave Rapide the petting of his life. We were joined by Mummy, Mrs. Derry, Ann's little sisters screaming with joy over Ann's green card, Mrs. Darcy and Captain Cholly-Sawcutt. Everybody made a fuss of Rapide who looked very smug.

'Did you see my April?' said Captain Cholly-Sawcutt. 'Wasn't she appalling?'

'You are really proud of her,' said Mummy, 'for being so plucky as to enter at all.'

'She's come on jolly well,' said Mrs. Darcy.

'In spite of being so fa –' began Ann, and shut up suddenly.

Class 2, open class, was just starting and we were very interested in what would happen to James and Wendy. Two walls had now been included in the course.

'Mrs. Woodhouse is sure to win it,' said Diana. 'She always looks as if she couldn't help winning.'

Mrs. Woodhouse and her horse were a lovely sight as they quietly and efficiently did a clear round.

'I think it's so depressing for the others when the first competitor does a clear round,' said Diana, thinking of James who was dithering on his new mare, Maureen. 'Who's going next? Oh, it's Berenice Wishford. She tells everybody that her horse let her down. I suppose it never occurs to her that she let the horse down.'

'Well, this one has run out with her,' said Mrs. Darcy.

'Oh look, it's Susan Pyke next!' shrieked Ann. 'In full hunting kit with white breeches. She looks about eighteen.'

'I hope she falls off,' said Diana. 'She's the biggest faller-offer in the world. She can't jump a horse that size anyway. Gosh! She *has* fallen off.'

'She'll get on again,' I said, but Susan got up limping, and leaving somebody else to retrieve her horse she retired.

'Isn't it lovely?' I said. 'Everybody we don't like is doing badly.'

'I think you're disgusting,' said Mummy.

Two or three men did good rounds and one of them, Major Pitts, got only two faults, but we weren't pleased as he was rude to other people and used his stick too much.

'Oh, it's James!' shouted Diana, and we all watched breathlessly.

But James was unlucky and did a bad round. Funnily enough the jumps he did brilliantly were the difficult ones and he got his faults at the ones which looked easy.

'I was awful,' he said despondently as he joined us, patting Maureen and saying, 'It wasn't your fault, old girl.'

'Your timing wasn't too good,' said Diana.

'For the love of Mike don't tell me!' said James.

'Stop arguing, you people,' said Mrs. Darcy. 'Wendy's started.'

Wendy was just clearing the second jump, and away she flew, her horse, Clarion, beautifully collected and taking the brook in his stride. It seemed only seconds before Wendy was coming up the hill, going steadily and confidently. She cleared the next two fences in lovely style, even the difficult one with the ditch on the landing side, and increased her speed for the last jump.

She's going to do it! I thought. Wendy's going to do a clear round!

Then a groan went up from the crowd. I shut my eyes, opened them again, and saw a rail of the last jump lying on the ground.

'Three faults,' said Mrs. Darcy. 'Well done, Wendy.'

'It's Mr. Brill, just coming up,' said James. 'He always does well, unfortunately.'

Mr. Brill was a very experienced rider on a long-legged grey, but today he was very slow and had several refusals, and though he cleared his fences the time limit expired before he got to the last jump and he was disqualified.

Nobody else did better than Wendy, and when they were called Mrs. Woodhouse was first, Major Pitts second, Wendy third, and a man called Harcourt reserve.

'I was certain I was going to fall off,' said Wendy modestly as we all pounded her on the back.

'None of the Lime Farm people have won anything,' said Diana with a lot of satisfaction.

She spoke too soon, because the next event, for novices, was won by Mrs. Drafter on a wicked-looking bay with a white blaze and docked tail. She did a clear round. However, we didn't care much, as everybody knew by now that the Drafters were leaving and that Mrs. Darcy had so many new pupils that she was buying more horses and taking on stable staff.

The only exciting thing about the novice competition was that James, on a borrowed horse, entered at the last minute and got the reserve. He and Wendy hadn't entered as they didn't possess second horses and it was too soon to jump Clarion and Maureen again, but a friend of James's father came to the rescue with an experienced chestnut called Frisk, and though James was nervous he rode beautifully and we clapped like mad when he was called in.

After that was the lunch interval, during which we fed the ponies and ourselves and talked about the events. The children's partnership was coming on immediately after lunch, and then the main event, the Swift Cup for horses that had hunted not less than three seasons.

'I'm scared blue about the partnership,' said Diana, who was riding with a girl called Gwen Snow. 'Gwen and I haven't practised together much, and Val and Jackie Heath have done nothing but practise together for weeks. It makes all the difference when the ponies are friends and will follow each other's lead.'

'Oh shut up,' said Ann. 'We're all equally bad anyway.'

When we were called into the collecting ring the steward explained the course. All the jumps except the in-and-out were too narrow for the ponies to jump together, as they do in pairs jumping, so we had to jump in turn, but the partnership had to be together when they reached the finishing post which meant that if you completed the course three jumps ahead of your partner you had to wait for her to catch up.

Diana said gloomily that she couldn't think of anything worse than Gwen standing waiting while she floundered in the brook three jumps back.

'You might still be floundering in the gorse at the first,' said James in a helpful brotherly way, as we waited for the first number to be called.

It wasn't very encouraging that the first round should be an excellent one, by Val and Jackie Heath. It was an education to watch their ponies co-operate, jumping nearly nose to tail, and finishing the course with only two faults between them and in an incredibly short time. I think they got the loudest applause the crowd had given that day.

There was a big entry for this event and some funny things happened as you can imagine. In one partnership of two sisters on a grey pony and a chestnut the grey could do nothing wrong and the chestnut nothing right. In the end both competitors finished up weeping. There were several violent rows too. One boy who finished the last jump far ahead of his partner went back and administered a sound slap to the other pony's flank, whereupon the laggard rider dismounted and pulled his partner's cap off and they fought. It was terribly unsportsmanlike but rather funny.

When it got to my turn with Ann I knew that at least I could rely on Black Boy who was very steady and experienced. I was a bit afraid for Ann's George

who was a nappy pony; Ann's mother liked nappy
ponies.

As I feared, George rushed his jumps and got two
ahead of me. I was so worried counting his faults that
I forgot Black Boy, and perhaps this was a good thing,
for my kind pony took control of the situation and I
found myself with a clear round. Ann had managed

to collect George by the time they reached the in-and-out, and finished with only four faults after all.

I had the feeling we might be in the running for a place, though the event went on for a long time as there were thirty-three entries.

Diana's fears were groundless and she and Gwen did a very good round.

When the judge called in, the Heaths and two brothers, farmer's sons called Bryce, both had clear rounds, but Jackie and Val were placed first as they had a lead of 11 seconds, and the Bryce boys second. Ann and I were third and Diana and Gwen reserve.

The big event of the day was coming up now, in fact a lot of the grown-up competitors had taken a dim view of having to wait until after the children's partnerships.

There were some magnificent horses and riders in the collecting ring, but our eyes were on Mrs. Darcy on Blue Smoke and Mr. Bush, James's father on Tiger Cub.

'Will you look at that!' said Ann, watching an enormous man being heaved into the saddle by a groom. His horse looked a real weight-carrier. 'Can you imagine that pair following hounds? They look as if they couldn't follow a tortoise.'

However, the fat man rode first and he certainly knew how to extend that grey of his. They lumbered home with only two faults and in quite good time.

Then we saw some really brilliant riding and I dreamed of a day to come when I too should be riding a hunter of three seasons in the Swift Cup. We all thought Mrs. Darcy was going to do a clear round on Blue Smoke until she knocked one block out of the second wall. Everybody groaned. Mr. Bush's horse was unfortunately in a refusing mood and he didn't do a good round, which we felt was a pity, as the Bush family were all skilled riders and should have taken something home besides two reserves.

Susan Pyke was entered on her father's hunter which, as usual, was far too big for her. She rode very showily and a lot of people clapped, but she didn't look so good when she finished the course with her arms round Matterhorn's neck and slowly clasping him like a necklace she slithered to the ground.

A man called Wilson who was a great comedian gave the crowd the laugh of its life. Mrs. Darcy said it was a pity that he would fool about as he was really an excellent rider and one of the best men to hounds in the county, only on an occasion like this he couldn't resist fooling. He pretended to fall at every jump and then recovered at the last minute, he made faces and pretended to be frightened, and finished up sitting in the middle of the brook while the crowd roared and he took his hat off to them. Some of the older people thought this exhibition was bad taste, but it certainly brightened things up and we were all helpless with laughing.

Then the master's wife, Mrs. Swift, did her round. This was sporting of her as she had no intention of taking a prize even if she won one in the event in which her husband was giving the prizes. However, she didn't stand an earthly. I think she was the slowest person round jumps I ever saw in my life and I couldn't imagine what happened to her out hunting. She crawled up to every jump as though it was going to say 'Boo' to her, she was quite prepared to allow her horse two refusals whenever he wanted them, she lost her top-hat and went to look for it herself instead of leaving it to a steward and when she had completed a jump she looked so overcome that she and her horse had to stand still and have a rest. However, everybody liked Mrs. Swift and when she finally finished, minutes after the allotted time when anybody else would have been disqualified, the crowd gave her a cheer and she looked beamingly happy.

'I suppose you realize,' said Wendy hopefully, 'that nobody has done a clear round?'

'Come to think of it,' said James, 'they haven't.

I believe Mrs. Darcy has a chance.'

In the end Mrs. Darcy and a man called Captain Tuft both had two faults. We stood on tiptoe and joggled about to see what was happening.

'Hooray!' yelled James like a foghorn. 'They're placing her first. Her time must have been better.'

Mrs. Darcy was first, Captain Tuft second and two unknowns took the next two places. We yelled with joy, and when Mrs. Darcy rode up to take the cup I should think the cheers nearly carried her along.

'What an absolutely wonderful day it has been,' said Ann.

Mrs. Darcy came up to us with the cup under her arm and we all crowded round Blue Smoke.

'I never thought I'd do it,' she said modestly, but you could see it was probably the most thrilling moment of her life. Then she congratulated us all on what we had done.

'And good luck to these two fellows!' she said, touching the cheeks of my Black Boy with his yellow rosette and Rapide with his blue one.

'Doesn't he look proud with his first rosette!' said Mummy. 'Dear old Rapide!'

'It's an extraordinary thing about Rapide,' I said, 'that he's a different pony now. He's completely changed his character.'

'Oh well,' said Mrs. Darcy nodding wisely, 'ponies sometimes do.'